MW00327175

Discover for yourself why readers can't get enough of the multiple award-winning publisher Ellora's Cave. Whether you prefer e-books or paperbacks, be sure to visit EC on the web at www.ellorascave.com for an erotic reading experience that will leave you breathless.

www.ellorascave.com

Ellora's Cave Publishing, Inc
PO Box 787
Hudson, OH 44236-0787

ISBN: 1-84360-392-6

Edited by Lee Haskell, Tina Engler, and Jennifer Martin
Anthology Lead Editor Karen W. Williams
Cover art by Bryan Keller

Warning:
The following material contains strong sexual content meant for mature readers. The Portal has been rated NC17, erotic. We strongly suggest storing this book in a place where young readers not meant to view it are unlikely to happen upon it. That said, enjoy...

The Portal

Warlord
by Jaid Black
-5-

The Seduction of Sean Nolan
by Treva Harte
-105-

Tears of Amun
by Jordan Summers
-175-

Warlord

by Jaid Black

Prologue

The Isle of Skye in the Scottish Highlands, 1052 A.D.

Euan Donald watched dispassionately as the decapitated body of the Hay fell lifelessly at his feet. Blood oozed out from where the laird's severed head had been but moments prior, pooling around him in a river of dark red.

Sheathing his sword, the Donald's dark head came up, his black eyes boring holes into the anxious faces of those Highlanders surrounding him. None would rebel. None would second-guess his decision to execute the Hay chieftain. None would dare.

'Twas not bravado on his part, not even ego. Not really.

'Twas simply the way of things, the territory that came with being the Lord of the Isles, the King of the Highlanders, a god unto himself. Euan's word was law, as it had always been, as had the word of his father, as had the word of his father's father, and so on.

At the age of five and thirty, Euan had been chieftain to the Donalds and Lord of the Isles for over fifteen years. The price of being the master of all he surveyed had been paid in full.

His six-foot-six-inch body was heavy with muscle and riddled with battle scars. The harsh angles of his face were chiseled into a stone-like façade and hinted at no compassion, no mercy for any who would come up against him. His eyes were as black as his hair, calculating pools of obsidian that broached no argument and conveyed no emotion at all.

To come up against the Donald was to die. This fact was one that kinsmen and Outlanders alike understood well.

Today, as he did on most days, Euan wore his plaid of muted blue and green, a large emerald brooch holding the material together at his shoulder. 'Twas a fitting banner for the man who ruled the Highlands with an iron fist...and who dwelled on an island many said was close to the heavens themselves, for it was surrounded on all sides and in all views by a formation of impenetrable clouds.

"'Tis done then." Graeme Donald, youngest brother to Euan, nodded toward a bevy of soldiers, indicating 'twas time to remove the Hay's bloodied carcass from the great hall. Turning to scan the nervous faces of the clan chieftains behind him, he waved a hand toward them and bellowed. "Will another amongst ye dare tae steal from the Donald?"

Murmured nays floated throughout the great hall, all eyes shifting from the Hay's remains to Euan's stoic form.

Graeme's upper lip curled wryly. "Weel then, 'tis time tae make merry, aye? Ye came fer a feast and a feast ye shall have."

Oppressive silence filled the chamber for a suspended moment. None were certain what to make of such an odd declaration. They had come for a wedding feast, every last one of them. They had journeyed from the protection of their respective keeps to witness marriage rites betwixt the Lord of the Isles and the first-born daughter of the Hay.

Not a one amongst them had ever fathomed the possibility that Tavish Hay would refuse to deliver the Donald's betrothed to her own wedding. Not a one amongst them would have credited the notion that the Hay would have been daft enough to allow Moira to break her sacred agreement and run off to the northlands with the brother of a Viking jarl.

For that matter, not a one amongst them would have been lack-witted enough to deliver such news to the Donald himself. Nay. They would have run hightail in the opposite direction. But then the Hay had never been renowned for his thinking abilities.

At last the laird of the lesser MacPherson clan broke the uncomfortable spell with a forced chuckle. "I will drink tae that." He lifted his goblet toward Euan. "Tae the Donald," he toasted, "and tae, err…" He shifted uncomfortably on his feet, the color in his face heightening. "Tae…"

Swallowing roughly, the MacPherson met Euan's black gaze. "Weel…" He lifted his goblet higher. "Tae the Donald."

"Tae the Donald."

The others were quick to chime in, all of them lifting their ales and meads in toast to the Lord of the Isles. Graeme's brows shot up, forming a bemused slash over his eyes as he cocked his head to regard his brother.

Euan smiled humorlessly as his dark gaze flicked from Graeme to the men standing behind him. Saying nothing, he stalked toward the dais that had been prepared for him in a slow, methodical stride. The great hall was so silent that each of his footfalls could be heard effortlessly, rushes on the ground or no.

When at last he reached the raised dais, he lifted the goblet that had been prepared for him and turned on his heel to face his rapt audience. Nodding once, he prepared to down the honeyed mead. "Aye," he rumbled, "I will drink tae that."

* * * * *

"What will ye do now, brother?"

Euan lifted a curious brow but said nothing. Standing atop the battlements, he scanned the outside perimeter below their position and absently awaited Graeme's meddling. His youngest sibling was the only in God's creation that could get away with such. 'Twas mayhap because he had raised him and felt him more a son than a brother.

Graeme waved a hand absently through the air. "Aboot getting wed, aboot siring an heir, aboot—"

"Graeme," Euan said quietly. "I'm no' lack-witted, mon. I ken your meaning."

Graeme nodded. "Then what will ye do?"

Euan shrugged. He had known three wives and had lost all of them to laboring his bairn. Out of all three pregnancies and subsequent fatal deliveries there had been but one survivor and that was his six-year-old daughter Glynna. After losing so many wives and babes, 'twas nothing, really, to lose a betrothed.

He turned his head to look at his brother, his facial features reflecting the fact that he had not a care one way or the other. A woman was a woman. Any woman of breeding years would do. "Get another wench tae take Moira's place in the bedsheets."

Graeme chuckled at that. "Mayhap had ye tumbled the Hay's daughter before the wedding she would have shown up."

One dark brow shot up. Euan shook his head slightly and looked away, his gaze flickering back down below the battlements. His hands fisted at his hips, the thick muscles in his arms bulged further in response. "I'm glad she dinna," he said honestly. "Truth be told I think a troll would be better bed sport than Moira."

Graeme grinned. "Ye have seen her before then?"

Euan shook his head. "Nay. But on Michaelmas three years past 'twas said by her own clansmen that she is possessed of an awkward appearance."

"I was no' there. That must have been whilst I still fostered under the MacPherson."

"Aye."

The brothers stood in silence for a long moment, breathing in the crisp night air. 'Twas May so the days were longer now, darkness still not having descended though it was well past the time of the evening meal.

Graeme's chuckle at last broke the silence. "I was thinking…"

"Hm?"

"Aboot the Hay."

Euan craned his neck to glance toward his brother. "Aye?"

"He owes ye a bride."

Euan waved that away. "I did no' kill the mon over Moira, though I know 'tis what the other lairds think. I killed him for betraying me. 'Tis a difference." He shrugged his broad shoulders. "Besides, the mon is dead," he rumbled. "His debt has been paid."

"No' really."

Euan sighed. It had been a long day and he was in no mood for conversing let alone for solving riddles. His youngest brother was mayhap lucky that he was able to rein in his temper where he was concerned. "Explain yourself."

Graeme thought to tease him a bit, but relented when he saw his brother's lethal scowl. He sighed. Why couldn't the man learn how to make jest? "As to that, 'tis true the Hay paid the price for helping Moira in her deceit, yet did he no' deliver another bride tae take her place in the bedsheets."

Euan grunted. "'Tis true."

Graeme stood up straighter, his back rigid with determination. "Then mayhap a wee bit o' reivin' might be in order."

"Reivin'? Ye want tae go steal some *cattle*?" Euan said the last incredulously. "'Twill no' even the score."

Graeme's face flushed at the criticism for which the Donald felt an uncharacteristic pang of sympathy. He knew that the boy had only been trying to help lighten his black mood. What his sibling seemed unable to understand on his own was that his mood was always like this. After ten and eight years the boy should know that. But he didn't.

Sighing, Euan forced a grin onto his face and ruffled Graeme's hair affectionately. "Ye are just wanting tae prove that ye learned things from the MacPherson more useful than merely how tae bed a wench. Aye, that's what it is I'm thinking."

Graeme chuckled, no longer embarrassed. "Mayhap."

Euan considered the idea more thoroughly before responding. Mayhap his brother was on to something. Not something quite like Graeme had envisioned — he hardly needed more cattle on Skye for the love of the saints — but something vastly more important. He did, after all, need a wench to take to his bed and get her with heir. Besides, as black as his mood had been as of late a bit of thrusting between a wench's legs was an enticement unto itself.

The Donald's black gaze flicked over the castle walls and toward the rock-strewn beach below. 'Twas not so long a boat ride to the mainland. And from there mayhap a sennight's journey to Hay lands at best. "I think," he murmured, "that ye might be right, brother."

Graeme's eyes widened in surprise. "I, uh, I…am?"

Euan couldn't help but to grin at the boy's astonishment. 'Twas true he wasn't a man known for changing his mind. Set in his ways he was. "Aye." He nodded, his demeanor growing serious. "We shall depart on the morrow when the sun falls."

Graeme smiled broadly, unable to contain his excitement. 'Twas the first reiving the Lord of the Isles had made him a part of, brother to him or no. 'Twas past the time to prove he was now a man and no longer a boy. "'Twill be a good time, thievin' the Hay's cattle."

Euan shook his head slowly as he met his brother's eager gaze. "'Twill no' be cattle we steal, boy."

Graeme's eyebrows shot up, forming an inquisitive dark slash. "The Hay's sheep are sorry I've heard it be told. No' verra wooly at all. Nay, brother. I dinna think their sheep are worth the time."

Euan shrugged. "'Twill no' be sheep we reive either."

"Then what? What will we be reivin?"

The Donald arched one arrogant black brow. His upper lip curled into a mirthless smile. "Wenches."

Chapter One

Nairn Scotland, Present Day

Eyes narrowing, Janet Duval's lips pinched together as she studied her outfitted form in the inn room's unflattering and depressingly accurate mirror. Nobody had ever accused her of being too skinny, she thought grimly, but lordy did she look pudgy in this number.

Twirling around to get a better look at her backside, she qualified that mental statement a bit. She didn't just look pudgy, she looked downright fat.

She wanted to go on a diet—really she did!—but she knew at the same time that she never would. Janet morosely considered the fact that her body seemed to be at its happiest when she was about twenty pounds heavier than what was considered cosmopolitan back home in the States.

Ah well. C'est la vie.

Unzipping the fashion monstrosity that she was supposed to wear to her business meeting tomorrow, she threw it into a pile on the nearest chair and fished around her suitcases for a comfortable sundress. Janet told herself as she climbed into the cotton, clingy number that nobody at the whiskey distillery cared one way or another how she dressed up for meetings anyway. So long as she showed up tomorrow with a hefty check and purchased a ton of

Highlander whiskey for the American-based firm she worked for, they'd all be happy.

After she'd donned the thigh-length, spaghetti strap green sundress, Janet took a speculative look at herself in the mirror and as usual found her attributes lacking. She wasn't gorgeous, she knew, but she oftentimes doubted that she was even remotely passable.

But then, Janet was the sort of female who would need a miracle before she'd realize her worth as a person and as a woman. Where Janet would have called her long, tawny-colored hair unremarkable, others would have noted the sleek beauty of it, not to mention the unruly curls that gave her a sensual, freshly bedded look.

Where Janet would have said her lips were too big and her smile too wide for her face, others would have thought her mouth lushly formed, her smile able to brighten even the blackest of moods.

Where Janet believed her body to be too fat for a man to get turned on by it, men conversely tended to think of her curves as fleshy and voluptuous, the kind of body a man could cuddle up with on a cold night and love until all hours of the morning.

But Janet Duval never saw that possibility. Never even considered it. Not even once.

Turning away from the mirror, Janet glanced about her private quarters in the local inn until she located her favorite pair of sandals. Stepping into them, she grabbed her cloak from a wooden peg jutting out from the bedroom wall just in case it got a bit chilly out.

It was May, that much was true, but even in May the Highland climate never surpassed the seventies. At night it could get downright cold.

Throwing her cloak absently over one shoulder, Janet picked up her purse and headed for the door. Tonight was, after all, fish and chips night at the local pub.

As she threw open the heavy door and closed it quietly behind her, she grinned to herself that no pudgy girl worth her salt would ever let a Scottish fish and chips night go by unattended.

Being pudgy might not be in vogue, but it beat the hell out of eating salad.

* * * * *

"Ach, Euan, I dinna ken why we are no' wearing our own plaids. Why must we sport these…" Graeme frowned as he swept his hand to indicate the nondescript, black garments they'd all donned. "…things."

Euan and Graeme's middle brother Stuart chuckled and answered the question instead. "Graeme boy, half the fun 'o reivin' is leaving the mon ye reived tae guess who it was that did it. Ye dinna wear your plaid like an emblem, dunderhead."

Defensively, Graeme's chin tilted upwards. "I knew that."

Euan shook his head at Stuart. He didn't think it wise to undermine the boy's pride before a dangerous activity. 'Twas mayhap only another few minutes' ride into the heart of Nairn, the village to where his riders had followed the Hay entourage.

'Twas luck, that. The Donalds wouldn't have to ride all the way into the eastern Highlands to abscond with Hay wenches after all. Soon they'd have their pick of the lot.

17

For whatever that was worth.

Euan nodded toward Stuart, indicating 'twas time to fall behind him in the line. Stuart acquiesced, nodding toward Graeme to do the same.

The predatory thrill of the hunt flowed into the Donald's veins, fixing his features into their usual harsh relief and causing his muscles to cord and tense.

'Twas time for the Lord of the Isles to find a wife.

Chapter Two

"Oh, Morag, you're terrible!" Janet shook her head and grinned at her best friend's story. She had met the rascally, redheaded Morag three years past when she'd first started working as the liaison between her firm and the whiskey distillery in Nairn. The duo had hit it off famously and had been inseparable ever since. "Did he really call it…" She wiggled her eyebrows and chuckled. "…a love hammer?"

Morag snorted at that. "Yea, he did. Can you imagine? That wee bitty thing…having the nerve to call it a hammer?"

Janet stretched her arms above her head as she yawned, absently thrusting her breasts outward. Many a man in the pub noticed and appreciated the view, but as usual, she was oblivious to their perusal.

Her green eyes sparkled playfully. "I've never seen it," she grinned, "but you've told me enough about it that I'd have to agree with you."

One red eyebrow shot up mockingly. "More like a love *pencil* I'd say."

The women laughed together, then moved on to another topic. Morag waved her fork through the air, punctuating her words as she spoke. "So are you going to take that promotion or no'?"

"I don't know." Janet sighed, her demeanor growing serious. "It would mean a great deal more money, but it would also mean that I wouldn't be traveling to Nairn every few weeks anymore. I'd be at corporate headquarters instead."

Morag's chewing ceased abruptly. Her blue eyes widened. "You wouldn't be coming to Scotland?"

Janet looked away. "No. Not very often."

"How often?"

She shrugged, though the gesture was far from casual. "Once or twice a year," she murmured.

"Once or twice a year?" Morag screeched. "Oh Janet, that's no' verra good news."

She could only sigh at that. "I know."

The women sat in silence for a few minutes, both of them lost in the implications of what it would mean to their friendship if Janet took the promotion her company was preparing to offer her. They'd hardly see each other. And they both knew it.

"Well," Morag said quietly, after a few more heartbeats had ticked by, "selfish or no', I'm hoping you don't take the offer."

Janet's tawny head shot up. She searched her best friend's gaze for answers. "What will I do if they fire me?"

Morag thought that over for a minute. "We've talked about going into business together more than once," she said hopefully.

"True."

Morag grinned. "Sounds like the perfect time to do it then."

Janet's lips curled into a wry smile. "I hadn't considered that option."

"Then consider it." Morag glanced down at her watch. "But consider it as we walk back towards the inn. I'm on duty for the late shift tonight."

"Oh, of course." Janet stood immediately, having momentarily forgotten that it was her best friend's job to run the small cozy inn her family owned and operated in the middle of Nairn. But then Morag didn't typically work nights. She only was this week because her brothers were off visiting friends in Inverness.

Janet didn't particularly care for either of Morag's brothers. In her opinion, they treated their twenty-five-year-old sister more like a worker bee than as a sibling and an equal partner in their deceased parents' heirloom of an inn. But Janet had never said as much to Morag. She figured if her friend wanted to talk about it, well, then she knew she was always willing and happy to listen.

The women paid their tabs and said their goodbyes to the other pub patrons, then made their way towards the door. Janet pulled on her cloak and buttoned it up after the brisk Highland winds hit her square in the face, underscoring the fact that the temperature had plummeted in the little time they'd been squirreled away inside the tavern.

"It's foggy out there tonight," Morag commented as she donned her own cloak. "More so than what's normal."

Janet studied the tendrils of mist with a curious eye as an inexplicable chill of uneasiness coursed down her spine. Shrugging off the bizarre feeling, she closed the pub's door and followed Morag outside into the dense cloudy formation.

"Yes," she agreed as they walked down the street. "It's strange out tonight."

* * * * *

"Morag," Janet said as her eyes struggled to penetrate the surrounding mist, "I can't tell which way is up let alone which way heads east toward the inn."

"Neither can I." She sighed. "Good God, Janet, this fog is like nothing I've ever seen before."

Janet nodded, though Morag couldn't see the affirming gesture through the swirling mist. The fog was so dense that the friends were holding hands lest they lose each other in it.

Janet looked left then right, but had no more luck seeing one way than she had seeing another. She used her free hand to burrow further into the cloak. Her heartbeat was accelerating, her skin prickling, and she wasn't altogether certain as to why. The fog was thick, yes, but that hardly accounted for the feeling of near panic that was swamping her senses. "We better be careful," she whispered. "We could run smack dab into a wall and not know it until it's too—*oomph.*"

"Janet!" Morag said worriedly, unable to see exactly what had happened. She only knew for certain that she'd come to an abrupt stop. "Are you all right, lovie?" When she didn't answer right away, Morag squeezed her hand tighter, urging her to speak. "Janet!"

"I'm fine." Janet giggled. "Remember how I said we could walk smack dab into a wall and not know it?"

"Yea."

"I did." She giggled again, her wide smile beaming. "Be careful, but come here and feel."

Morag pivoted slowly in a circle, allowing her best friend to lead her slightly to the right and place her hand on a cold stone wall. She chuckled when she realized that, indeed, Janet truly had walked into a wall. "This will make for a good story." She grinned, her eyes at last finding Janet's through the layers of mist. "I can't wait to tell everybody about—"

A shrill scream pierced their ears, abruptly bringing a halt to whatever Morag had been about to say. Their eyes widened nervously.

Janet's tongue darted out to wet her suddenly parched upper lip. "D—Did you hear that scream too?" she said in an urgent tone beneath her breath.

"Y—Yea." Morag swallowed a bit roughly as she glanced about.

Squeezing her best friend's hand, Janet attempted to steady her breathing, but found that she couldn't. "We must leave here," she said, her heart feeling as though it might beat out of her chest. "But I can't see which way to go."

"Neither can I," Morag murmured. "Oh God, Janet, there's another scream!" she whispered in a panic.

"It wasn't the same as the first." Eyes rounded in fright, Janet used her free hand to clutch the wall that was now beside her rather than in front of her. She sucked in her breath when her hand didn't come in contact with a stone wall as it should have, but with a wall that felt as though it were made of…earth and twigs?

"What the hell?" she asked herself almost rhetorically. "Morag, this wall isn't right!"

Morag didn't know what to make of such an odd declaration, so she ignored it. "Come. Behind the wall," she whispered. "The fog does no' look so thick back there."

Janet glanced toward where her friend was pointing and nodded. She said nothing as she retreated a few steps backward, stepping behind the wall she had just clutched, a wall that looked to belong to a home of some sort. Only that couldn't be right. Homes in the Highlands were no longer made of thatch, and they hadn't been for years and years.

Shaking her head, she thrust the odd feelings at bay and followed quietly. Only when they'd gained their position did she speak. "The fog seems to be lessening a bit," she whispered.

Wide-eyed, Morag nodded. "That could be good or bad, I'm thinking."

"I know." Janet squeezed her hand and breathed deeply to regain her composure. She could be of no help to either Morag or herself if she wasn't thinking clearly. "If the fog lifts we'll be able to see who's causing the screams, but..."

Morag closed her eyes and said a quick prayer to Mother Mary. "They will also be able to see us."

"Yes."

Morag closed her eyes again to finish her prayer, leaving Janet to keep vigil.

Not even a moment later, Janet watched in horror as the fog lifted a bit and the surreal scene before her revealed a large barbaric-looking man clamping his palm over a young girl's mouth and lifting her up into his overly muscled arms. He passed the girl to another man mounted atop a horse, only then glancing over in their direction.

Janet shuddered as her large green eyes made contact with piercing black ones. She tried to clutch Morag's hand tighter, only then remembering her friend had released hers to say a prayer. "Shit," she whispered frantically, "he sees us."

"Oh my God," Morag cried out, "we've got to—"

Morag's scream caused Janet to whirl around on her heel. She watched in helpless horror as a mounted rider flew by on horseback and snatched Morag off the ground with one sweep of a heavily muscled arm. Tears of overwhelming fright gathered up in Janet's eyes. In shock, she drew her arms around her middle and hugged herself as she listened to Morag wail for her to go get help.

Help. Yes, help...

The reality of the fact that there was aid to be found within running distance helped to snap Janet from her state of frozen shock long enough to get her to move.

She would get help for Morag. *Oh God...Morag!*

Pivoting on her sandal, she turned toward the enveloping mist, preparing to dash into it, uncaring of the fact that she would be nearly blinded, unable to see through the thick fog. Braving one last glance over her shoulder, she clamped her hand over her mouth when she heard Morag's scream and watched as her best friend's captor held her securely while riding off to only God knows where with her.

Janet's gaze was drawn toward where the lone dismounted man stood, the largest and most frightening looking of all these marauders. He was watching her, seemingly undisturbed by the fact that he knew she was about to run.

She sucked in her breath as his black gaze found hers and his lips slowly curled into a terrifyingly icy smile.

Saying a quick prayer of her own, she broke his stare and fled into the mist.

Chapter Three

Janet ran as fast as her feet would carry her. She sprinted at top speed toward…anywhere. She had no clue as to where she was going. She could see nothing, hear nothing, feel nothing that wasn't associated with acute fear.

The cold didn't matter. The fact that she'd tripped at least twice already and had skinned up both of her knees didn't matter. The only sight she could conjure up was the mental image of Morag's abduction. The only sounds she could hear were the beating of her own heart and the gasps of air her lungs sucked in as she struggled for each breath.

She'd been running for what felt like hours but had only been minutes. She dashed through the fog, refusing to slow down no matter how weary and pummeled her body felt. She might never make it to help before she was murdered on the streets of Nairn, but she'd be damned if she wouldn't go down trying.

Pumping her arms back and forth as her body trod through the boggy mist, she let out a small whimper of relief when she noticed a break in the fog just ahead. Dashing toward it with everything she had left in her, she came to an abrupt halt once she reached her destination.

"Oh my God," she muttered in between pants. Her eyes darted back and forth, taking in the bizarre scene around her as she doubled over to catch her breath. "Where in the hell am I?" she rasped out.

Janet's mouth dropped open in morbid fascination as her eyes flicked about the row of crude mud and thatch huts that she'd wandered into the midst of. She'd never seen anything like them. Well, she'd never seen anything like them outside of lands that had been preserved for their historic value, she mentally amended.

Snapping out of the reverie that had swamped her, she took a deep breath and reminded herself that she needed to find some sort of help. Morag was in danger. God in heaven, she thought hysterically, her best friend had literally been kidnapped off the streets! She could only hope Morag's captor didn't force himself on her—or kill her—before she could be rescued.

Steeling her nerves and forcing herself to behave with a calm she was far from feeling, Janet took a tentative step out of the mist and toward the row of thatched huts just ahead. She *would* get help. For Morag she would find a way.

Janet tried with every fiber of her being to make that mental vow a reality, but before she could take another step from the fog, a heavily muscled arm whipped out and snatched her back into the eerie cloud formation. She opened her mouth to scream, but was forestalled from carrying it out by a large, callused hand clamping roughly over her lips and grinding into her mouth.

Frightened and quite certain he meant to kill her, she bit down as hard as she could on whatever skin she could find, bearing down until the metallic taste of blood trickled onto her tongue.

It wasn't enough. The small nick she'd given him hadn't even caused him to flinch.

Flailing madly about, she gave him her full weight then, hoping it would induce him to drop her long enough to allow her precious moments to make good on another escape. Anything—even a single moment's hesitation on his part—and she'd try to flee into the mist again.

But that wasn't to be. When Janet's feet purposely shot out from beneath her and she tried to fall buttocks-first toward the ground, the same heavily muscled arms that had caught her in the first place merely swept her back up as though she were a rag doll. He whirled her around to face him, his large hand still clamped over her mouth.

"Seall dè fhuair mi," he said in a chillingly controlled tone. "Nach e tha mear."

Janet's green eyes rounded uncomprehendingly as her head shot up. She'd never heard such a language. It sounded vaguely similar to the Gaelic she'd heard some of the Highlanders in these parts speak and yet so different at the same time.

Breathing rapidly, her heart rate over the top, Janet determined to look up—way up in fact—and meet her captor's eyes. He might kill her, and was no doubt preparing to do so, but she'd be damned if she'd act the coward while taking her last breath.

She was afraid to look at him, terrified in fact. She'd never encountered a man so huge, so powerfully built. The arm he had wrapped about her felt as heavy as a tree trunk, so roped with muscle it was. He was shirtless, making it easy to ascertain the fact that his equally massive torso was riddled with…battle scars?

Janet sucked in a deep breath from behind the giant's hand and, casting her fears behind her, shot her gaze up to meet her captor's dead-on. And then she wished she hadn't.

His black eyes drilled into hers, piercing her with a possessiveness she'd never before witnessed, never experienced. The look he was bestowing upon her was so primal that it terrified her.

He didn't mean to simply kill her, she now knew. No. Escaping him would never be that easy. He meant to have her, to rape her.

Janet's last coherent thought before falling into the first faint of her life revolved around whether the barbarian would choose to kill her before, after, or…*during*?

And then the blackness overtook her and she thankfully knew no more.

* * * * *

Euan held onto the wench's middle as her limp body sagged against him atop the destrier. 'Twas just a wee bit further they'd go before making camp for the night, getting their party as far from the scene of the reivin' they'd just done as was possible in a night's journey. The Hay would definitely retaliate. He planned to be on his own lands when they did so.

Graeme had been right after all, the Donald thought in a rare flash of humor. The reivin' had been a spot of good fun.

As he ran his hand over his future bride's plump breast and felt a nipple pop up through the fabric of her finely made outer tunic, he conceded that he'd especially enjoy reaping the benefits of tonight's coup. He could scarcely wait to rut between his wench's legs. His manhood was painfully erect just thinking about it.

Euan absently toyed with the nipple, plumping it up between his forefinger and thumb as he considered where the closest village with a priest might be located.

He wouldn't fuck her wee body until he owned it by law, so he'd have to make certain she was his posthaste.

The Lord of the Isles would be made to wait but so long.

Chapter Four

"Janet, wake up. Please, lovie, please...*wake up*."

Janet could hear Morag calling to her from somewhere in the back of her mind. But everything was so hazy, so obscured. Her best friend's voice seemed miles away. Her eyelids felt heavy, the muscles of her body were on fire, her knees felt as though someone had raked them across a serrated blade.

"Janet, *please*...please wake up."

Black eyes. A man. Morag's screams.

The night's activities slowly began to unravel in the fogginess clouding her brain...

But she'd gotten away! She'd fled into the mist for help. For — Morag. *Oh God...Morag!*

But no. The man had stopped her. The battle-scarred...warrior? A warrior?

"Janet, for the love of Mary would you open your eyes." This in urgent tones from Morag.

Morag? Morag was here? She'd gotten away? Oh...Morag!

Ice-cold water pelted Janet in the face, waking her up instantly. She bolted upright, sucking in huge gasps of air, the frigid liquid shocking her into alert mode.

She blinked a few times in rapid succession as her eyes took in the strange surroundings. Animal hides enclosed her on three sides, the bark of a large tree on another. The tiny space she was sitting in consisted of earth and animal furs.

A tent. She was sitting in some sort of primitive tent. Her gaze clashed with Morag's. "Where are we?" she whispered.

"Oh, lovie," Morag said as she ran a hand through Janet's mane of unruly tawny curls. "I didn't think you'd ever wake up."

"I'm fine." Janet sat up straighter and forcibly shook the remaining cobwebs from her brain. "I'm awake. Morag, what's going on? Who are those men? Where have they taken us?"

"I don't know." Morag worried her bottom lip as she threw a long red tress over her shoulder. "I can no' understand a bloody word of what they are saying to me, Janet. These men..." She lowered her voice and leaned in closer to her best friend. "These men are dangerous. We must run away!" she said urgently. "Preferably *before* they come back to interrogate us again!"

"Interrogate?" Janet's eyes widened. "They've interrogated you?"

"They've tried." Morag sighed. "Janet, they can no' understand what I am saying to them any more than I can comprehend what they are saying to me."

"How can that be?" Janet shook her head slightly, more confused than she was frightened, which was saying a lot. Her gaze darted back toward Morag's. "That makes no sense."

"I know." Morag was quiet for a pregnant moment as she studied her friend's features.

"What, Morag? What is it?"

"It's just...it's..."

"Yes?"

She sighed. "Janet, something verra strange is happening here. Something…something isn't right."

Janet was surprised she was able to find a chuckle amidst the chaos, but she did. "No kidding," she said wryly.

Morag didn't return her mirth. "I'm serious, Janet. I do no' just mean the fact that we were kidnapped in the heart of Nairn by a bunch of over-large, non-English speaking men. It's…it's…more than that." She took a deep breath and glanced away.

Janet clasped her hand and squeezed it. She had felt those same odd premonitions since she'd first laid eyes on the fog when they'd trekked out of the pub. "Tell me," she said under her breath. "Tell me what you think is going on."

Morag nodded, deciding to waste no more time. "Bear in mind before you dismiss my musings as nonsense that I have been awake since this entire sordid mess began. I have seen things you have no' seen, or things you have no' seen yet anyway."

Janet's heartbeat picked up. Her skin began to tingle as it had back in the mist. She didn't have any idea what Morag was about to say, but whatever it was she knew she wasn't going to like it. "Go on."

"These men…" Morag's eyes widened as her voice dropped. "These men are no' like any men of our acquaintance, Janet. Their bodies are covered in battle scars, they ride upon horses instead of in cars." She waved a hand through the air. "They carry swords and wear almost no clothing save scratchy blackish plaids, for the love of Mary!"

Janet drew her knees up against her belly and wrapped her arms around them.

"We traveled on horseback for hour upon hour last evening and no' once, *no' even once*, did I see a home of normal appearance." Morag began to shiver. She rubbed her arms briskly, warding off the chill. "Every last home I saw with my verra own eyes—every last one, Janet!—was made of thatched twigs and clay."

"Like something out of a history book?" Janet murmured. She closed her eyes briefly, remembering only too well the row of thatched huts she'd run into before the gigantic dark-eyed man had captured her.

"Yes," Morag said shakily, "just like something you'd see in a history text, or on a tour of preserved relics. Only people *live* in these relics."

Janet sucked in a deep tug of air. Her lungs burned, felt heavy. "So what you are saying," she rasped out, "is that…"

No! Things like that don't happen!

"What I'm saying," Morag continued for her, "is that…" She looked away, couldn't go on.

Janet closed her eyes. "…That we've traveled through time."

The words hung there between them, feeling more than a bit strange on the tongue and yet, perversely, feeling more than a bit right as well. Morag was the first to speak. "Well," she murmured, "as fantastical as it sounds, I for one do no' think we are in our own time any longer."

Janet's eyes flew open. She blew out a breath. "You sound quite calm about such a terrifying possibility."

Morag shrugged helplessly. "I've had more hours awake to deal with all of this than you."

"True," Janet murmured. She searched Morag's eyes as she considered for the first time since she'd awakened just what else her best friend might have seen, might have been made to endure. "Morag..." Her throat felt dry, parched.

"Yes?"

"The man who took you. Did he...I mean..." She stumbled over her words, unable to find the right ones. "Did he..."

"No." She shook her head. "He fondled me a wee bit, but he did no' rape me, thank the lord."

Janet released a shaky breath. "Thank God for that at least."

"But he will," Morag said quietly. "They mean to do with us what they will, Janet. Make no mistake." She shivered. "The way the fairer-headed man looks at me, the way I saw that brutal-looking black-haired man staring at you..." She let her words trail off portentously, not finishing her sentence.

"Shit." Janet drew her knees in closer to her body. "What do we do?"

"We escape."

"But how?"

Morag found her first chuckle. "I have no' got that far in my plans."

Janet snorted at that. "And if our time travel theory is correct and we are indeed existing in some prehistoric, barbaric era..." She shook her head slightly as her gaze found Morag's. "Then what good is escaping? Where will we go?"

Morag nodded definitively. "Back toward Nairn."

Janet raised a brow as she considered that. "Good idea. Maybe that weird fog will still be there and we can get back home."

"Exactly."

"Or maybe this is just a dream."

"Maybe."

Janet sighed. "But you don't think so."

"No." Morag shook her head. "I do no' think so."

The women stared at each other until Janet broke the silence. "Well then, the only thing left to figure out is how we get out of this…" She flung a hand towards one animal pelt wall. "…thing."

Morag chuckled softly. "Unfortunately, that will be the most difficult part to figure out." She patted Janet reassuringly on the knee, causing her to wince. "But we— oh dear, what's wrong? Is it your knee, lovie?"

"Yesss," she hissed as she sucked in air between her teeth.

"Let me see." Morag undid the buttons of Janet's cloak, carefully tugged it open, and quickly ascertained how bad the situation looked. Since Janet was wearing a sundress that only came to mid-thigh while standing, it rode up even further while sitting, making it easy to see that her knees were badly skinned up. "Ouch." Morag winced sympathetically. "I take it you got scraped up whilst running?"

"Yes. I—"

One of the animal pelt walls flapped open and the figure of a brooding, dark-haired man emerged. Janet's heart rate picked up, pounding inside of her chest. The women huddled closer together, a natural reflex given the situation.

The giant's gaze sought out Janet's, but was snagged a moment later by the sight of her naked leg. She swallowed roughly in reaction as she watched the barbarian study the thigh most adjacent to him. His eyes trailed from the knee upward, slow and lingering, his gaze burning into her so hotly that she hysterically wondered if a cattle brand would magically appear on her leg. Why not? Everything else about this situation was insane.

He wanted her. She'd be a fool not to see it. His burning eyes said so. His meandering gaze said so. The thick erection poking against the kilt-like, blackish covering he wore said so. She averted her gaze and quickly looked away.

The heavily muscled giant stood there for another moment before making his way further into the tent. His movement caused Janet's head to snap up and her body to huddle impossibly closer to Morag's. The warrior noticed her reaction and, oddly enough, slowed his movements down, approaching her in a manner that was surprisingly non-threatening for one so large and obviously lacking in gracely finesse.

Everything about the battle-scarred man spoke of command and authority. He was a warrior accustomed to taking what he would when he would. And yet he approached Janet cautiously, the way an adult would when trying to lessen the fright of a skittish child.

Their gazes clashed when his large, callused hands were placed softly on her knees. Janet's eyes widened nervously. She glanced toward Morag, who was shaking like a leaf, then back to the warrior squatting before her.

One hand slid slowly down her right thigh, the leg opposite the side Morag was sitting near, so her friend didn't know what the stern-looking giant was about. His grim black eyes were glazed over with desire as he trailed his hand gently over the expanse of her warm, soft flesh. He touched her as though he couldn't seem to help himself, as though there was nothing in the world he wanted or needed more.

Such a response from a man might have been an aphrodisiac under normal circumstances, but under the current ones it was gut-wrenchingly frightening. Janet began to swallow convulsively.

Her reaction didn't go by undetected. Again, at odds from the warrior's harsh exterior, he showed her the kindness of dropping his hand from her thigh and settling it back upon her skinned knee. His eyes sharpened almost instantly, as if he had momentarily forgotten himself but was now back in control.

And then he was preparing to leave. Just like that. He dropped his hands from her knees and stood up from his squatting position.

Janet couldn't help but to notice how heavily muscled his legs were when they flexed into standing mode. Indeed, the warrior's entire body was so formidably carved it looked almost god-like.

Janet watched him exit the tent, watched as the animal skin flapped shut behind him, then cocked her head to gawk at Morag whose own jaw had dropped open. "What was that about?" she whispered.

"I don't know." Morag swallowed a bit roughly. She squeezed Janet's hand. "I—I thought he meant t—to…"

Janet breathed in deeply. "So did I. I—"

The tent flapped open again and her gaze clashed with the warrior's. His mask was back on, that stony impenetrable façade that she would have thought he always wore had she not witnessed that blazing look in his eyes a minute prior.

Her green eyes widened noticeably as he lowered his powerful thighs before her and squatted between her legs once again. Her breathing became shallow and choppy as she prepared for the worst.

Would he rape her right here in front of her best friend? Would Morag be made to watch so she'd know what was in store for her as well? The mere thought of such humiliation caused tears to form in her eyes.

Large, callused hands thrust her legs open a bit wider. Janet looked away, fighting back tears of fright. She could feel Morag's breathing growing labored as they both prepared for Janet's assault. Morag cried out softly as the warlord settled himself intimately between Janet's thighs.

No! Janet thought hysterically. This couldn't be happening! Please God...

Janet closed her eyes and bit down hard on her lip. The metallic taste of blood trickled onto her tongue. Her heart was beating so rapidly she could hear nothing but the pulse of it. She squeezed Morag's hand as she felt his breath come closer.

And then she felt *it*—the hardness of his erection brushing up against her leg from beneath his coarse wool covering. Panting almost hysterically, Janet clamped down on Morag's hand as the warrior placed...

A wet rag on her knee.

A wet rag on her knee?

Confused, Janet's eyes flew open and clashed with the giant's. Her breathing slowed so rapidly it halted completely for a lingering moment. The warrior was…good lord, he was tending to her wounded knees!

Eyes rounded, she looked quizzically at the giant who didn't seem to notice her. He was busy patting icy cold rags on her knees, tenderly wiping away the dirt that had mingled with the blood on her exposed, raw flesh.

Flicking her eyes toward Morag, Janet couldn't help but to notice the bemused expression on her best friend's face. It was that of a deer caught in headlights. Clearly, she had assumed the battle-honed giant had meant to harm her as well. Playing nursemaid was the last thing either had expected of this formidable man.

Janet's gaze slowly raked over the giant's austere features. He wasn't a bad looking man, she admitted to herself. In fact, if she'd met him under any circumstance other than the one she currently found herself in she would have found him superior in appearance.

His features were grim, but handsome. Hair black as midnight flowed a bit past the shoulders and was swept out of his eyes by a Celtic braid plaited at either temple. His eyes were dark, so brown they almost looked black. She noticed for the first time that the iciness of his gaze was lessened somewhat by sweeping, inky black eyelashes that formed an impressive crescent when his eyes were shuttered as they were now while he studied her knees.

She shouldn't be noticing these things, she told herself stiffly. The warrior might be showing her a kindness by tending to her wounds, but they were wounds his pursuit of her had caused in the first place. She was, Janet reminded herself, no more than a prisoner to him. She asked herself, not for the first time, just why she and Morag had been captured to begin with.

Her inward musings were brought to a halt when the warrior finished his task and began to speak. His voice was a deep bass, the richest rumble she'd ever heard. She definitely didn't understand a word of what he was saying though.

"Madainn mhath. Ciamar a tha thu?" His black gaze swept over her breasts, settled on her face.

Janet pretended not to notice his perusal of her anatomy. She shrugged and answered his question with a perplexed look.

He tried again. "Dè 'n t-ainm a th'ort, te bheag?"

Her green eyes merely grew larger. She glanced toward Morag, then back to the grim-faced warrior. She shook her head slightly, again shrugging her shoulders in a helpless gesture. "I don't understand your words," she said quietly.

Comprehension dawned in the giant's eyes. They widened almost imperceptibly before he re-commanded them and the façade was neatly back in place. He seemed to turn things over in his mind for a moment or two, then pointed to himself and rumbled out a word. "Yu-an."

Janet shook her head, not understanding.

He pointed toward himself again, thumping a callused hand in the vicinity of his chest. "Yu-an."

She was about to shake her head again when the significance of the giant's actions at last dawned on her. Euan. He was telling her that his name was Euan.

Glancing first toward Morag whose rounded eyes indicated she still hadn't caught on, she looked back at the warrior and pointed toward herself. "Ja-net."

"Joo-nat." His deep voice repeated her pronunciation — sort of.

She didn't know why, but she felt the need to correct him. "Jaa-net," she said louder, more distinctly. She pointed at him. "Yu-an." She pointed back toward herself. "Ja-net."

He smiled, giving him a somewhat softer appearance. A dimple popped out on his left cheek, which Janet found oddly fascinating. "Jah-net."

She nodded, then smiled in spite of herself, weirdly elated by the fact that they'd managed that small communication, no matter how insignificant, and no matter that she was still his prisoner.

* * * * *

Euan walked from the tent feeling more than a wee bit daft. The purpose of yester eve's reiving had been to steal Hay women. The comely wench was clearly not Hay, mayhap not even Scottish. So why did he think to keep her regardless?

He shook his head and sighed as he strutted toward the campfire where his brothers and men awaited him. Wenches did strange things to men. Especially wenches who sported creamy thighs and fleshy bosoms.

He came to a halt in front of his siblings, then nodded toward Stuart. 'Twas Stuart who had caught the redheaded wench and had a wish to keep her. "'Tis as ye suspected, brother. The wenches do no' speak our tongue."

Graeme chuckled, earning him a punch in the side of his jaw from Stuart. That didn't hold back his mirth, though. "At least my fair Elizabeth kens what I say tae her."

Stuart rolled his eyes, then looked back to Euan. "Ye are certain?"

The Donald nodded briskly. He thought back to the conversation that had just taken place in the makeshift tent.

"Madainn mhath. Ciamar a tha thu?" Good morning. How are you?

Nothing.

"Dè 'n t-ainm a th'ort, te bheag?" What is your name, little one?

Again, nothing.

"Aye," he confirmed, grinning a bit at the memory of he and Janet pointing toward themselves and pronouncing their names as slowly as lack-wits. He quelled the small smile, his features quickly shifting back in place. "I dinna ken from where they come, but 'tis sorely apparent they do no' comprehend a word of what I'm speaking tae them."

Stuart grunted. "I dinna care, brother. I want tae keep the fiery-haired wench." He wiggled his eyebrows and grinned. "I'll teach mah wee bride Gaelic betwixts thrusts in the bedsheets."

Now it was young Graeme rolling his eyes. He decided to ignore Stuart. "What of ye, brother? Will ye keep the other one?" He nodded toward Euan as he considered her appearance. "She is comely for a certainty."

Euan grunted as he shook his head wryly. "Aye. And one hell of a good runner."

A few of the soldiers surrounding them laughed at that.

Stuart grinned. "'Twill no' be easy tae chase your wench down long enough tae thrust, brother. 'Twill mayhap be a while before that bride learns Gaelic."

The laughter evolved into gaffaws. Euan acceded to it good-naturedly, uncharacteristic though it might be.

The Lord of the Isles needed an heir and therefore a wife. Janet was the comeliest lass he'd ever laid eyes upon. Big, sparkling green eyes. A lush bosom. The sort of fleshy body he could lose himself in, pumping away into oblivion. His mind was made up. Why bother looking elsewhere when perfection was already awaiting him in yon tent?

"Aye," Euan rumbled. "I will keep her."

"Then ye best get busy." This from Graeme.

Euan lifted one dark brow.

Graeme grinned, then bowed mockingly toward his elder siblings. "Your comely wenches?"

"Aye?" they asked in unison.

Graeme jerked his head toward the tent where even as he spoke two women were emerging, making efficient beelines toward the thick of the forest, dashing off into it at top speed. "I dinna think they ken the honor ye give tae them, making them Donald brides." He chuckled. "In fact, looks tae me as though they are getting away."

Chapter Five

Janet glowered at the giant brute standing beside her, one bulging and vein-roped arm plastered about her waist. So much for her ill-fated escape attempt, she thought glumly. The only thing it had garnered her was *his* undivided attention, not to mention being forcibly separated from Morag as though they were two naughty girls being grounded from playing with each other by their fathers.

So now she stood beside her captor who, much to her disgruntlement, looked extremely handsome now that he'd cleaned himself up a bit. Frightening, but handsome nevertheless.

He was wearing a clean plaid of muted blue and green with a white tunic beneath it. His plaid was draped over one arm and held together by a large emerald jewel at one shoulder. The garment fell just above his knees, showing off legs too well muscled to belong to a human.

Janet's lips pinched together. It wasn't fair that a man so dastardly should look so good.

Men who had the look of soldiers began to gather in on all sides. At first Janet thought it was to make certain she didn't try to flee — as if she could with Euan's tree of an arm clamped around her! — but now she wasn't so sure. They didn't seem to be paying her much attention, in fact. Their interest seemed to lie with the short little man standing in front of her and Euan, the one wearing a scratchy looking robe with a hooded cowl and speaking in some other foreign tongue she couldn't make heads or tails of.

Janet sighed. It had been a long day. It felt like days ago that she and Morag had attempted to fly the coop so to speak, but in reality it had only been what was probably ten to twelve hours.

After they had been recaptured, Euan and the fair-haired man that had stolen Morag had separated the women from each other's company. They'd been within seeing distance of the other at all times, but not within a range that allowed for conversation.

Janet had managed to scrape up her knees even worse while on the run, tripping over the fallen branch that had eventually permitted the big oaf at her side to catch up with her. Damn branch.

Following her rather ignominious recapture, Euan had re-cleaned her knees in private then shut her cloak. He had pointed and growled at her clothing, making it apparent that she wasn't allowed to remove her outerwear for any reason whatsoever.

Not that she would have. She hardly wanted to show off skin to any of the men surrounding her.

Following his grunts and stern finger-pointing lecture, Euan had placed her atop a horse and jumped up to sit behind her on it. They had ridden that way hour after hour, stopping only briefly to eat and care for the animals.

If there had been any lingering doubts in her mind as to whether or not she and Morag had managed to do the inexplicable and travel through time, they had quickly been vanquished during the horseback ride. There was no evidence of the modern age anywhere to be found.

Nothing but horses, non-English speaking peoples, shabbily dressed villagers, the occasional man or woman hawking crudely made foods and wares, and wild animals galore.

Then they had come to this place. This hole-in-the-wall village that boasted a few thatched huts and little else. Morag had been the first to be swept from her horse and squirreled away into the very forest clearing Janet stood in right now.

When Morag had emerged from the clearing a bit later, her face had been white as a ghost's. She had been trying to tell Janet something with her eyes...something, but what, she hadn't any notion.

Janet's gaze had fallen to Morag's clothing. The cloak she wore hadn't looked torn or bore any evidence of a man trying to rip through it to force himself on her. That had been Janet's primary concern. When that fear had been wiped away, she'd been left in a quandary, knowing full well that her best friend had been trying to warn her of what would transpire in the forest clearing, but still unable to figure out what that something was.

So now here she stood, soldiers surrounding her on all sides, Euan stoically planted to her left, a tiny Latin-speaking man just in front of her. Latin? Yes, come to think of it, his words sounded remarkably like Latin.

The smallish man produced a bolt of cloth, placed Janet's hand atop Euan's, and wrapped them together like that. Curious, Janet's gaze shot up to meet Euan's. He didn't return it. His solemn face was intent on whatever it was the Latin speaker was saying.

What was going on! she wailed to herself. If she even knew what time she was in she might be able to sort out all of these strange happenings...

"Tha." Euan nudged her gently, breaking her out of her reverie. "*Tha*," he repeated commandingly, nodding down to her so she'd know she was expected to repeat what he'd just said.

Janet's eyes widened as a sense of awareness slowly stole over her. *Tha*. She'd heard that word before in the Highlands. It meant *yes*. If she repeated it, what exactly would she be agreeing to?

She nervously moistened her lip with her tongue, in the end deciding that there was no point in arguing with the man. If he wanted a yes she'd give him a yes. Begrudgingly, she narrowed her eyes at Euan and phonetically repeated the word she'd been prompted to say. "Ha."

Almost immediately the Latin speaker followed up with a few more words of his own. He said...something. Something that made Euan smile for a fraction of a second before he lowered his face to hers and kissed her chastely on the cheek.

Congratulatory shouts rose up from the surrounding soldiers, many of them thumping the giant beside her on the shoulder, almost as if they were saying to him "job well done."

Janet chewed that over for a moment.

How odd...

She stilled. Her back stiffened. Her eyes shot up to meet Euan's as she gaped open-mouthed at him.

His answering arrogant smirk was all the confirmation she needed.

Good lord in heaven, she thought. The man had just married her. And worse yet, she'd agreed to it.

Chapter Six

Janet stood inside the crude hut where Euan had cloistered her just short of an hour past, morosely wondering if this pathetic place was to be her new and permanent home. The hut boasted but one room…one single, solitary room. A hay-strewn bed lay at one side of it, a kitchen-like area with a few clay bowls on the other, and a solitary chair in the middle.

That was it. No tables. No more chairs. No anything. She hated it immensely.

Naked, Janet covered her breasts with her hands as best she could while she watched two village women remove the crudely made tub she'd just bathed in from the one-room hut. She nibbled on her bottom lip, hoping that the women would hurry up and come back with her clothes. She didn't want to be caught unawares when her husband returned.

Her husband. Janet groaned. Good lord! How would she ever get out of this mess, find Morag, return to Nairn, *and* get back to the future? The task set before her was simply overwhelming.

The wooden door opened a moment later causing Janet's head to shoot up. Her breath caught in the back of her throat and her eyes widened skittishly when she realized that the new occupant was not one of the village women that had helped to bathe her, but instead the very man she least wanted to see while naked.

Dusk was just beginning to settle over the Highlands, so there was still enough light to notice the heat in Euan's eyes as his black gaze raked insolently over her body. He was erect, very erect, she could easily surmise, his stiff penis bulging against the plaid he still wore.

He quietly closed the door behind him and slowly made his way towards her. Janet sucked in her breath and took a reflexive step backwards.

Euan stopped in his tracks, approaching her cautiously again, just as he had in the tent before tending to her knees. It was then that she noticed he carried a platter of some sort. Food. Against her will, her stomach growled hungrily in reaction to it.

"Hai." He dipped his head. His blazing gaze raked over her flesh once more, lingering overlong at the clipped tawny curls between her thighs. But he made no move to touch her.

"Hi," she whispered back. She gnawed on her lower lip and looked away.

It occurred to Janet that it was stupid to stand there shielding her breasts from his view when her mons was completely bared to him. But nonsensical or not, she continued to cup them.

Part of it was borne of fear, knowing what he meant to do to her and knowing equally well she wouldn't have enough physical power to stop him when he did. But she had spent all day long with him, first while he tended to her knees and then again for the long trek on horseback to the rugged area of the Highlands they were now in. She was afraid of him, yes, but not as acutely as she'd once been. He treated her too tenderly to fear him overly much.

No, it was definitely more than fear that kept her hands cupping her breasts. It was also reflex, Janet's naturally shy reaction to standing totally divested of clothing in front of a male.

Back home in the States she had endured all manner of teasing as a child and then again as an adolescent. Pudgy. Plump. Fat. Fluffy. Big-boned. Piggy. She'd heard every derogatory term imaginable coupled with her name, every euphemism there was to express the fact that she wasn't a rail and would therefore never be as desirable as every woman wanted to be to the opposite sex.

But this man, she told herself staunchly, this man had captured her, had made her his prisoner, had taken her against her will...had even married her, for the love of God! If he wasn't happy with the end result, that was his own doing. Perhaps he'd even let her go once he realized his mistake.

Firmly resolved to get it over with while she was still angry enough to do it, she dropped her hands from her breasts and defiantly thrust her chin up. Her nostrils flaring, she stood there and waited for him to reject her.

His reaction wasn't quite what she had been expecting.

Euan groaned, the fire in his eyes raging brightly, licking over every lushly rounded curve, every nuance of her fertile figure. He didn't seem at all put off by her body. In fact, he gazed at her with such obvious desire that Janet's nipples involuntarily puckered up for him and her breath caught for the briefest of moments.

Biting her lip, she glanced away, shaken by both of their reactions. Now what did she do? She'd feel like an idiot re-covering her breasts at this point.

And then the decision was taken away from her as she heard him put down the platter of food and come to her. Two large, callused hands cupped her breasts and gently kneaded them like soft dough. He plumped them up with his hands, taking the nipples in between his thumbs and forefingers, and massaged them from roots to tips.

Janet closed her eyes and gasped. "No. Please. No."

From somewhere in the back of her mind it occurred to her that her voice sounded smoky with passion, not defiant with anger and fear. Euan didn't speak her language, she reminded herself, as he massaged her breasts and nipples into a deeper state of arousal. If she wanted him to understand that his touch wasn't welcome, she'd better sound more forceful about it.

Janet's green eyes flew open and locked with Euan's black ones. He continued to stroke her, to tug just the right amount on her nipples—just enough to where it didn't hurt, but sent tremors of desire coursing through her blood.

She opened her mouth to say no, but found herself sighing and her eyes glazing over instead.

He was handsome. Incredibly, impossibly, muscular and virile. The sort of man that would never look twice at her in her own time, but for some reason or another was fascinated by her in this one.

This was—*madness*. She couldn't even speak with him, couldn't converse with him, knew nothing about him beyond the fact that his name was Euan and he was well versed in tending to wounded knees…and other things.

One of his hands dropped a heavy breast and a callused finger found the sensitive piece of flesh between her thighs and stroked it. "Oh God," she breathed out.

Janet's head dipped back, her neck bared to him, all rational thought out the proverbial window. "Oh God."

Where a minute ago she would have tried to say no, she found in this moment that her feet were moving apart to give his hand better access to her clit. She closed her eyes against her worries and fears, accepting the pleasure, and moaned softly.

It was all the impetus Euan needed to further his ministrations. "Mmm, tha," he rumbled, his eyes watching her face as his hand cupped her flesh and felt her pussy getting wet for him.

And then he was lifting her into his arms and carrying her to the bed. He sat her down on the edge of it and splayed her legs wide.

Janet offered him no resistance, opening them impossibly wider for him, so that her labia were on prominent display. The entire scene felt surreal, like it had to be happening to any woman but her. A more brazen woman. A more wicked woman. Not the reserved and mousy Janet Duval.

He traced the slick folds of her flesh with one callused finger, the look on his face reminding her of someone who'd found the most glorious treasure on earth and wanted to explore every facet of it. His reaction to her body was heady enough to induce her nipples to pop out further as desire shot through her at lightning speed.

"Oh lord." He was rubbing her flesh again, stroking her clit, exploring every wet nook and cranny. Her head dangled backwards like a puppet. She leaned back on her elbows and splayed her legs as wide as they would go. He began to rub her more briskly, faster and faster. "*Euan.*"

"Mmm, te brèagha," he rasped out.

Beautiful one. He'd called her *beautiful one.* She'd understood that, knew that expression from her friends in Nairn. Her breathing grew more labored with each touch.

Faster. Faster.

Oh God, the stroking was faster, brisker...faster still. *"Oh god."*

She was soaking his hand, saturating his fingers. And still impossibly faster. *"I'm coming Euan."*

"Tha, te brèagha," he urged her on. *Yes, beautiful one.*

He didn't need to understand her language to comprehend what words she was groaning out. Her body was telling him.

"Euan," she moaned. *"Faster. Yes...God – faster."* On a final groan, her head snapped back, her nipples shot out, and her labia turned a juicy red as her orgasm blew. Blood coursed into her vagina and nipples, heating her body, burning her face.

And then he was coming down on top of her...already naked? She didn't know when or how he'd discarded his plaid but didn't care either. She made him do a little groaning of his own when she pulled him roughly down on top of her and wantonly wrapped her legs around his waist. She wanted him to fill her – needed him to fill her.

Euan clenched his jaw as he poised his thick cock at her entrance. If she didn't slow down a wee bit he was liable to do her damage. "Gabh do thìde," he gritted out. *Take your time.*

But she was wild for him, his beautiful wee wife. Hot and wild. He'd never experienced such a primal reaction from a wench, had never seen a woman filled with such passion as his Janet. He was gladder than ever that he'd snatched the wrong wench for a wife.

Instead of slowing down, she gyrated her hips, thrusting them upward towards his jutting cock. It was his undoing. There was only so much a man could take, the Donald or no.

Grabbing her by the hips, he thrust deeply inside of her tight, wet flesh, groaning like a man possessed as he did so. Christ but he'd never felt anything so tight and welcoming.

"Oh, Euan."

She was breathing out his name in her passion already, he thought with more than a little arrogance. Grabbing his wife's large, elongated nipples, he settled his body atop hers and began thrusting into her in long, deep strokes. He rolled the nipples around with his fingers, tugging at them in the way he'd discovered she liked.

"Faster."

She groaned out that foreign word over and over again. As much as he wished it otherwise, Euan knew not her meaning. He continued burrowing into her in long, agonizingly languid strokes.

"Faster," she all but shouted, this time arching her hips to pummel at his cock in quick strokes.

Ahh. Now *that* he understood.

Euan released his hold on Janet's breasts and came down fully on top of her. Twining a handful of her long, sweetly scented hair around his fist, he locked gazes with her just before he rammed himself home.

She groaned, her head falling back upon the bed as he rode her body hard, fucking her sweet cunt in fast thrusts. "Tha domh phuiseag fearachdainn math," he said hoarsely. *Your pussy feels good.*

Sweat-soaked skin slapped against sweat-soaked skin. The sound of Janet's sweet cunt sucking up his manhood reverberated throughout the shepherd's hut.

Euan growled as he went primal on her, fucking her harder and faster, riding the body he now owned by law into ecstasy and oblivion.

"Euan."

His name on Janet's lips as her back arched and her body climaxed for him was powerfully arousing. She shivered and convulsed, moaning wantonly as she burst all around him.

In one fluid movement, he grabbed her hips and rammed himself inside of her body, over and over, again and again. Quick strokes. Deep thrusts. Flesh slapping flesh.

His muscles corded and bunched. His jaw clenched. He rode her fast, hard, like an animal. "*Leamsa.*" *Mine.*

And then he burst.

Nostrils flaring, Euan's black gaze collided with Janet's as he thrust home once more, then on a groan of completion, spurted himself deep inside of her.

They held each other like that, both of them spent and breathing deeply, both of them too exhausted and replete to speak.

Euan bent his neck to sip gently from her lips. Janet accepted him without hesitation, sweeping her tongue out to meet with his. They kissed slowly for a minute or two, sweet and languid brush strokes until their mingling stopped completely.

Entwined with each other in every way possible, they fell fast asleep.

Chapter Seven

She woke up to the feel of a tongue sliding along the folds of her swollen flesh. The tongue was tantalizingly rough and slick, rimming her labial folds with precision, flicking across her clit, rimming, flicking, rimming, flicking...*god.*

She moaned in reaction, her eyes not yet opened, her brain still drunk on pleasure and sleep.

The tongue was joined by firm lips, lips that closed over her swollen clit and helped the tongue to suckle her. Flick, suck, flick, suck, flick, suck...*oh yes.*

She ground her hips to meet the tongue and lips as her nipples stabbed up high into the air.

Flick, suck, flick, suck.

Suck, suck, suck, suck...*Euan.*

Janet's eyes flew open and her hips flared upward on a groan as she climaxed into his mouth. *"Oh god."* Instinctually she wrapped her legs around his neck and buried his face further into her flesh, wanting him deeper, needing him to suck her dry, wanting the pleasure-pain to never relent.

"Mmmm." He lapped at her like a dog, slurping up the juices that trickled out of her engorged flesh, then sucking again — harder, torturously harder until —

"Oh my god." Janet reared up off the bed, screaming because the pleasure was so acute. *"Yes, Euan."*

Reflexively her body tried to disjoin from his mouth, uncertain it could handle falling over such an all-consuming precipice of pleasure. Euan grabbed her hips in reaction, simultaneously shoving his mouth deeper into her cunt and suckling from her clit harder.

"Oh Jesus god. Oh my...god!"

Janet's hips tried to thrash about, but he held her steady, not letting go, never relenting. "Mmmm," he growled, vibrating her clit all the more. His sucking became merciless, faster — harder.

Her head flew back, her nipples hardened and elongated impossibly further, blood rushed to her face. *"Yes...oh yes!"*

And then she was there, falling over the precipice, screaming from the ecstasy, wanting more, needing filled and fucked.

Euan flipped her over with a growl as he came to his knees, wanting to take her from behind on all fours. "Dinn," he gritted out, nudging the back of her head gently.

Lying on her elbows, Janet looked over her shoulder and made a face, not understanding. She arched an inquisitive brow at him.

"Dinn," he stated with more force, again nudging her head. His eyes were blazing, his muscles corded, his thick cock jutting and swollen. "Dinn."

Janet's lips formed an O. He wanted her upper body pressed down further. She complied readily, spreading her legs far apart, sliding off of her elbows and pressing her head and torso further towards the bed, her buttocks and labia dipping upward for his use.

He grunted arrogantly then cupped her labia from behind and pressed his palm and fingers upwards. "Suas."

That must mean "up," she told herself wryly. Her face heating up despite the night they'd already shared together, Janet submitted, keeping her head and torso down while simultaneously thrusting her labia and buttocks up into the air as high as they would go.

It was a wicked feeling, she thought, being on display like a man's personal whore. But when Euan expelled his breath on a groan while running his hand over her exposed flesh, she decided that wicked could be a good thing.

"Leamsa."

He growled out that word again, the word he had used the last time he'd fucked her, the word he was even now repeating over and over again as he rubbed her wet flesh.

Mine. Janet somehow understood that leamsa meant *mine.* Her body reacted to his possessiveness, her nipples hardening and her breath quickening.

"Leamsa."

She gasped as he impaled her, her flesh slurping up the impressive length of his cock, her labia reflexively arching skyward for more. He gave it to her.

Euan gritted his teeth as he slid in and out of her, thrusting into her depths in long, penetrating thrusts. "Leamsa."

"Oh god."

He pummeled faster, pounded harder, thrust into her to the hilt. Over and over. Again and again. "Leamsa."

The slapping sound of her soaked flesh sucking up his cock reverberated, grew louder and lustier as she grew wetter and wetter. "Leamsa."

Janet thrust her buttocks back towards him, meeting each of his thrusts as he gave them to her. The harsh jiggling of her breasts caused her already sensitized nipples to grow that much harder. "*Euan*," she moaned out. "*Oh god...Euan.*"

She buried her face in the bed furs as her body began to convulse, her pussy contracting around his steely flesh. She half screamed and half sobbed from the pleasure, so powerful was her orgasm.

"*Leamsa*," he roared possessively, his jaw clenching. His callused fingers dug into the flesh of her hips as he thrust faster and faster, harder and harder. His muscles were tensed, the veins in his neck and arms bulging, his balls impossibly tight from the need to burst.

Janet moaned, continuing to meet his thrusts with thrusts of her own. "*Yes, Euan*," she groaned, "*god yes.*"

And then she was coming again, pulsing around him again, contracting again, moaning like a mortally wounded animal because the pleasure was so acute as to border on the painful.

"Tha, te bheag," he gritted out, "taom a-mach e." *Yes, little one. Pour it out.*

"*Oh god.*" Waves and waves and waves of pleasure shot through her, jutting out her nipples like hard gems, heating her face like a furnace, sending her over a cliff of sensation.

"*Leamsa*," he growled definitively, slapping into her deeply for a final thrust. Gritting his teeth and closing his eyes, he groaned as he erupted, spurting his seed deep inside of her.

A suspended moment later, when the intensity had died down a bit and some sense of rational normalcy settled in, Janet began to wonder why Euan was still holding onto her hips, thereby forcing her buttocks and labia to remain skyward. Confused, she drew herself up as far on her elbows as he would allow, then glanced over her shoulder to study his face.

The mask was back, that stone cold façade that broached no argument and allowed no leniency. And yet, conversely, his black eyes blazed more possessively than she'd ever seen them before.

A chill of foreboding swept through her, causing her eyes to widen and her throat to parch. He was about to do something — or say something — and she had no idea what. All she could do was wait. Sit there on all fours, her labia on display for him, and wait for whatever it was that he was about to command.

And then his large, callused hands were reaching under her and grabbing her breasts. He found the nipples, pinched them between his thumbs and forefingers, and locked gazes with her. "Leamsa," he said softly. Too softly. He tugged at them a bit so there would be no mistaking his meaning. "Tha?" *Yes?*

Janet's eyes widened further.

"*Tha?*" he asked more sharply, pinching her nipples again.

He wanted her to say it. He wanted her to acknowledge his ownership of sorts over her. She hesitated for a moment, uncertain as to what she should do. She didn't want to stay in the past, no matter how enjoyable these past few hours had been.

Eventually, however, the look in his eyes scared her into nodding. She would not say the word, but she would nod.

When she submitted Euan released one nipple, then used his free hand to trail down to the soaked and swollen flesh between her thighs. He slid two large fingers in her to the hilt, then met her gaze once more. "Leamsa," he murmured, his deep voice a rumble of authority and power. "Tha?"

She nodded briskly.

"Tha?" he asked again, louder, angry now.

She nodded again, assuming he hadn't seen the small gesture.

"*Tha?*" he bellowed, thrusting his fingers in again and pinching one of her nipples.

Janet's eyes widened nervously. He wanted her to say it—aloud. He wouldn't settle for anything less.

She swallowed harshly as her gaze clashed with his for a final time. Clearing her throat nervously, she nodded once more. "Tha," she agreed quietly.

With an arrogant grunt, he began to massage her clit with one hand and the nipple he was still latched onto with the other. She groaned, her head falling limp as he rewarded her for her compliant answer.

And then he was impaling her all over again and Janet thankfully had to concern herself with rational thought and worries of ownership no more.

Chapter Eight

Janet had been surprised when Euan had awoken her a few hours later, indicating that they were going to depart this place where they had shared so much passion together. He had taken her again, thrust himself into her with a groan as though he couldn't seem to help himself, as though her body was the most soothing place in the world for him to be. He had brought her to orgasm at least twice, maybe three times. She had been so groggy with pleasure and peaking she could no longer remember.

Euan had given her a new dress then, a floor-length green number that was not only quite beautiful, but also more appropriate for his world. She could only assume that he'd somehow acquired it during the bath she'd taken after he'd married her.

And then he had taught her several new words by leading her outside and pointing to various things. He had been patient in his instruction, which had surprised her. She didn't know why she was surprised really, for he'd been extremely gentle with her ever since he'd captured her.

Perhaps she'd been taken aback because of the way Euan bellowed orders at his men. She'd quickly surmised that he was the leader amongst the group for everyone catered to him efficiently and unquestioningly. If he barked out a command, it was obeyed and answered instantly. It was through these exchanges that by the second day of their journey from the village Janet found herself picking up more and more words from Euan's tongue.

Janet was pleased that she seemed to be learning key words and phrases from his language rather rapidly. Not enough to where she could yet carry on meaningful conversation—they'd been together but three days after all—but enough to where she was slowly beginning to comprehend what he meant without his having to point at whatever word or action he was trying to describe.

The past three days had felt much like a dream to Janet. Riding through the Highlands on horseback, the brisk winds hitting her in the face, stopping to look at the wares of the occasional nomadic craftsman, making camp—and making love—with her husband at night.

Her husband.

The knowledge that she even had a husband, let alone one that had died hundreds of years before she'd been born, was what felt more surreal than anything else. And weirder still, she wasn't altogether certain how she felt about it.

Three days ago Janet would have escaped Euan at the first opportunity. Today, if given the choice, she wasn't certain what she'd do. Such an admission was not only startling to her, but terrifying as well.

And Morag—oh how she missed Morag. Janet had no idea at all as to how her best friend was faring. Morag and her captor, a man Janet could safely assume was now Morag's husband, had ridden out ahead of she and Euan the morning following the weddings.

Where Morag had been taken Janet couldn't even begin to speculate. Worse yet, she wasn't well versed enough in Euan's tongue to put such a higher-level question to him. It was one thing to be able to ask for food and drink, quite another altogether to express feelings and concerns. She felt as though she were floating along like a piece of driftwood, unable to control her own destiny and uncertain as to where the waters would lead.

On the fourth day of their journey their entourage had been attacked by a group of bandits that outnumbered their party three to one. One minute Janet had been eating an apple as she rode in front of her husband on his mount and the next she was startled into dropping the piece of fruit by the sound of ear-piercing war cries followed by the thunder of hooves as a group of sword-wielding men assaulted them from the south.

Wide-eyed, her gaze had shot up to Euan's. He had paid her no attention, dashing off toward a tree with thick, high branches instead, and placing her into it for safekeeping while he'd galloped back to charge directly into the fray.

Janet had been frightened. Not only for herself, but for Euan as well. Tears of frustration and terror had welled up in her eyes as she'd watched him ride off, watched him engage in a fight in which the numbers greatly out stacked any hope of a Donald victory.

A Donald. Janet now understood that her last name was Donald, or MacDonald. Apparently the two names were interchangeable, but since she knew from her own time that "Mac" meant "son of," she could assume that in these times the "Mac" was dropped as redundant, leaving whatever name was behind it to stand solo.

Not that she'd thought about something as inane as name trivia as she'd watched the skirmish unfold. She had considered the naming business later on, after the Donalds had surprised her by quickly vanquishing the threat to them.

It had been chilling, watching her husband kill men before her very eyes, watching as his heavily muscled and vein-roped arm bore down on men with such force that his sword had neatly sliced through their now dead carcasses like butter.

He had worn that mask again, that stony façade that was so much a part of him...a part of him that was always in place save for the moments of passion they claimed together at night. But she supposed such a mask was necessary in this world, a needed way of severing all emotion from whatever job had to be done in order to keep your wits — and life — intact.

And so now here she stood on the fifth day of her journey, gazing out into the frigid Highland waters from shore as she watched a large boat being made ready for them to take them to...well she didn't know where precisely, could only conjecture from the bits and pieces of Scottish history she'd gleaned while working in Nairn.

Janet knew that the clan MacDonald heralded from the Isle of Skye, that tiny dot of an island in the Hebrides where a man known as the Lord of the Isles had ruled as a king of sorts over the Highland clans in medieval times. She could only surmise, therefore, that since her husband's last name was Donald, or MacDonald, Euan must be of this lord's direct clan.

Janet felt tired and bone-weary from their long journey. And she was confused, still overwhelmed by everything that had taken place this past week. And what's worse, at least to her way of thinking, was that she deeply suspected she was beginning to grow feelings toward her husband that she wasn't particularly interested in having. Attached feelings. Caring feelings. Feelings of…love.

It was just that he was so…good to her. Euan made her feel special and loved and desired—three things she had never felt for a man back in her own world, most likely because no man had ever felt them for her either. The way he looked at her, the way he held her as though he'd never let her go or let anyone take her from him…it was heady stuff. Heady stuff that had little by little evolved into a deeper affection for him.

But how did he feel for her? she wondered. It was hard to speculate when she wasn't well versed enough in his language to speak with him! But, Janet thought somewhat nostalgically, it was only when looking at her— just her—that his mask slipped from place, and bits and pieces of what in any other man would have been termed vulnerability could be seen.

Leaning against the bark of a tree, Janet had closed her eyes for barely a moment when the feel of soft lips placing kisses on her mouth startled her into opening her eyes. She kissed him back without qualm, then smiled up at the gentle giant towering over her. Well, gentle might not be the best term used to describe him, but he was gentle towards her at any rate.

Euan didn't smile at her, but then he never did. She could see the affection for her in his eyes though, the way they seemed to sparkle whenever he looked at her—and only when he looked at her. "Ciamar a tha sibh?" he asked somewhat briskly.

Janet cleared her throat a bit, answering him in broken Old Gaelic. "I am well. How are you?"

"Good. We will travel tae my lands today."

She looked at him quizzically.

"Land," he repeated quite patiently. He stomped his foot on the earth below him and repeated the word. "Land." When her eyes lit up with comprehension, he grunted, his usual response when pleased with her ability to learn quickly.

"We will go on the boat?" she asked him, pointing toward the large wooden vessel in case she was using the wrong word.

Apparently she hadn't. Euan nodded, speaking slowly so she'd understand him. "Aye, we will. 'Twill take most of the day."

Janet noticed that he didn't seem terribly put off by such a notion. And then she understood why when he backed her up against the tree bark and pressed his erection into her belly. The glazed-over look in his eyes coupled with his thick erection let her know in no uncertain terms just what he planned to do with her to while the hours away on the boat.

"Mmm, Janet," he murmured against her ear, "I need tae love ye."

Janet's body responded immediately, her nipples hardening and her breath catching. She knew her own eyes were glazed over, could feel them narrowing. "Yes," she whispered.

And then Janet did something she never would have been bold enough to do to a man in her own time. Reaching up under his plaid, she wrapped her palm and fingers around his thick cock and began to masturbate him.

Startled, though not unpleasantly so, Euan sucked in his breath. "Ah, Janet." He closed his eyes, clearly trying to steady himself, and pushed at her hand. "Stop," he said gruffly. "Later, wife."

But Janet wasn't listening. She felt empowered by the response he always gave her, brazen and daring.

Euan was given only a moment to wonder at the mischievous look suddenly in his wee wife's eyes, his own nearly bulging from their sockets when she dropped to her knees and her head disappeared beneath his plaid. Right here under a tree. Where anyone could walk upon them. She was massaging his balls underneath his plaid.

"*Chan eil,*" he hissed under his breath. *No.*

But again, Janet wasn't listening. She'd never done this for him before and suddenly she wanted to do it more than anything on earth. She took him into her mouth, sucking from tip to base, deep-throating him in one suck. She was elated when he gasped in astonishment, then acquiesced to her on a low moan.

Obviously this wasn't an activity women of his time knew much about. Good, she thought wantonly. The realization that for once he was more of a virgin in this arena than her made her all the more determined to bring him to orgasm.

"*Janet,*" he said harshly, a disembodied voice from where she couldn't see him on the other side of the plaid.

And then she was pumping him in and out of her mouth in quick sucking strokes, letting his cock go almost the entire way out of her mouth before suctioning him back in with her lips and tongue. She knew the smacking sounds of her suckling were as much a turn-on to him as they were to her.

Janet realized the exact moment when Euan mentally capitulated. His breathing ragged and choppy, he thrust the plaid from around her so he could watch his cock disappear into the depths of her mouth and throat. He groaned at the wicked sight, his muscles cording and tensing. "Aye, Janet," he said hoarsely. "Dinna stop kissing me."

Grabbing her by the back of the head with both large hands, he helped to ease himself in and out of her mouth, riding her faster and faster, much as he did to her pussy while mating.

Janet gave him everything, holding back nothing. She sucked him hard, faster and harder, in and almost out, over and over, faster and faster. Kneading his tightly drawn scrotum with both hands, she suckled on him relentlessly, knowing from his now incessant moaning that he was about to burst.

"Tha, Janet," he gritted out between pants, his jaw clenching as he continued to ride her mouth, "doit mo bhod." *Suck on my cock.*

And then he was coming, riding her hard as he spurt into her mouth, moaning louder than she'd ever heard him moan before, uncaring if anyone heard what they were about.

Janet drank of him, sucked every drop of him dry, until his cock once again lay flaccid and sated in the nest of dark curls at his groin.

Euan drew her up to her feet, hugging her tightly against him, as if thanking her.

* * * * *

Five hours and three blowjobs later, Janet decided that she had created a monster. Her jaw was sore, she was slightly seasick from the rough movement of the waters in a postage-stamp sized cabin that boasted one tiny bed of animal furs and a few small slits for breathing in oxygen, yet she couldn't seem to stop herself from obliging his carnal longings.

Clearly, Euan was enthralled with the new form of pleasure she'd introduced to him. He hadn't left her side once. Not even to go check on the voyage's progress.

Three times now Janet had fallen asleep with a sated cock in her mouth and three times she had been awaken to a stiff, thick erection poking at her lips, wanting entry. She always gave it to him, of course, then secretly smiled when she'd hear her husband moan as he closed his eyes and lay back to enjoy a special treat.

Janet honestly didn't know how her jaw was withstanding so much sucking, but it was. Every time she got sore to the point where she didn't think she could carry on, it took but once glance toward Euan's face to change her mind.

His expression while she sucked on his cock reminded her of what she assumed a little boy who'd discovered masturbation for the first time would look like — gloriously enraptured. A man who had found and captured Nirvana.

* * * * *

Euan simply could not get enough of his wife's suckling. He knew he was being hard on her poor mouth, but he kept awakening from his slumber with a rock-hard erection and a new load of juice that needed relieved. And by the saints, 'twas bliss the way Janet relieved him. He'd never before experienced such a sinful delight.

"Ah, Janet," he murmured, as he watched her beautiful mouth slurp up his cock, "keep kissing him," he groaned. "Dinna stop, love."

Love. Not a word he'd expected to feel for his wife. Not a word he'd felt for any female save his daughter Glynna.

Nay. With Janet he had felt lust upon seeing her, more lust than he'd ever entertained in his life. Lust that had driven him to capture her twice, lust that had speeded him towards the first village with a priest just so he could rut inside of her, lust that had kept his cock hard and pumping his cream into her more often than he'd believed to be possible.

But somehow over the course of the journey back home, over the course of fucking her mindless and spewing inside of her several times a night, the Lord of the Isles had fallen in love with his captured bride.

He would never let her leave him. Never.

Euan sucked in his breath and groaned as Janet released his cock from her mouth and bent lower to suckle of his man's sac. Running his fingers through her long curly hair, he closed his eyes and enjoyed the bliss.

Nay. He would never let her go.

Chapter Nine

The castle was beautiful. Janet simply couldn't get over how gorgeous it was, a mythical looking place that was probably no more than a shell of a relic in her time if indeed it still stood at all. Honestly, she didn't know. Although she'd heard a great deal about the Isle of Skye, she'd never actually visited it. But she was here now. And wow was it awesome.

The entire island was the most lush, picturesque place she'd ever laid eyes on. Emerald green grass, true blue skies, fragrant bluebells that stood at attention in the wind. It was breathtaking.

And the castle—simply indescribable in its wonder. She gawked at the fireplace in the great hall where she was currently standing, taken aback by how large it was. She would easily be able to stand upright in it and still have a bit of headroom. It was that tall. And the width—twenty replicas of her could stand side by side in it. She imagined it took a great deal of kindling to light so massive a structure every day.

And then there was the little girl. Glynna, if she'd understood Euan correctly. She was roughly six years in age and about the prettiest little thing Janet had ever laid eyes on. There was no doubt as to who had fathered this child. If the jet-black curls and stubborn jaw hadn't given away her parentage upon first glance, then the way she'd flung herself into Euan's arms upon seeing him certainly would have.

What's more, it was obvious that the father was deeply in love with the daughter. Euan had actually broken into a full smile upon seeing Glynna, bending down, scooping her up off the floor, and affectionately rumpling her fine coif of a hair-do.

Janet had smiled while watching, mesmerized by the sight of it. She'd always wanted children, but she had never thought she'd have one. She didn't know how she felt about having one now. Latching on to Glynna, a motherless little girl who even now was holding her hand as she stood next to Janet and watched her father order this man and that man about, was paramount to all but giving up any hope of returning to the life she'd known but a week ago.

But did she want to return? Janet wondered silently for at least the fiftieth time. What was there for her really, especially with Morag here in the past? A job she was probably going to get fired from? An empty apartment in Cleveland she rarely saw?

There was no man in her former world that was special to her. No family either, for that matter. Her parents had been dead for over five years, killed in a diving accident three days before Janet's twenty-second birthday.

Neither did she boast any real friends in the future save Morag—Morag, whom she still had yet to see. She was beginning to worry that she'd never see her a—

"Janet!"

Wide-eyed, Janet whirled on her heel at the sound of that very welcome voice. Smiling brightly, she continued to clutch Glynna's pudgy little hand as she opened her arms and giggled when her best friend came bounding into them. "Morag!" she laughed.

"Oh, Janet!" Morag hugged her tightly. "I was so verra worried for you!"

"I'm fine," she promised, hugging her back. "But what about you? How are you?"

Morag released Janet and stepped back a bit. It was then that she noticed Glynna for the first time. She smiled down to the little girl. "And who is this?"

"Glynna," Janet answered.

"Euan's daughter?"

"Yes."

Glynna smiled, displaying neat white teeth. "Hallo, milady," she whispered very sweetly in Old Gaelic.

"Hallo," Morag answered back with a grin, apparently having learned about as much of the tongue as Janet had. "You are verra pretty, Glynna."

"Thank-ye."

Janet's brow furrowed. Obviously Morag had learned a bit more of the tongue than she had. She reverted back to English. "How did you know those words? And how did you know Euan's name?"

"Stuart."

"Stuart?"

"Yes, Stuart," Morag responded. Her cheeks pinkened a bit as she cleared her throat. "My, uh…"

"Husband?"

She nodded. "I tried to tell you that day in the forest but—"

"It's okay," Janet said wryly, "I pretty much figured it out for myself."

"Among other things, I'd wager."

Janet shook her head. "What's that supposed to mean?"

Morag chuckled. "We were in the same boat as you and your husband, you know, even if the men would no' let us see each other until we docked."

"And?"

She grinned. "Your man was doing more than a wee bit of moaning from what I could hear all voyage long."

Janet's face flushed with heat. She couldn't hold back the small smile that tugged at the corners of her lips though. "So glad I was able to unknowingly provide entertainment," she murmured.

Morag smiled, chucking her playfully under the chin. "Quit blushing. You have the look of a turnip."

Janet happened to glance down just then and noticed that Glynna was watching a little girl across the room play with a doll. The look in her eyes was one of unadulterated longing, a child desperately wanting to play, yet she made no move to dislodge herself from Janet's side even though it was obvious she'd rather be doing little girl things.

Good lord, Janet thought, she'd never met a child so in control of her naturally playful and exploratory nature. Not a good thing at the age of six, to stand off to the side rather than indulge. She turned to Morag. "Do you know the word for 'play?'"

"Hmm." She thought that over a minute, then threw a word at Janet.

Janet nodded her thanks then turned back to Glynna. "You may play now if you would like." She smiled down to her.

Glynna's return smile was so big as to border on bursting. Janet now understood that when Euan had first brought the little girl to her side, he must have instructed her to remain with Janet unless told otherwise. Good grief, how boring for a six-year-old!

"Thank-ye, mum."

Janet's back stiffened. She hadn't been expecting such an endearment so soon, if it all, and she was confused as to how she should feel about it. It was frightening. And yet heart-warming at the same time. Realistically she knew the little girl was probably only calling her by the name she'd been told to use, but it didn't keep her heart from swelling up just a bit. "You're welcome," she said softly, scooting her gently away from her skirt. "Go play now."

Morag chuckled as the little girl bounded away. "She is a verra pretty wee thing."

"Mmm yes. She is."

The conversation turned then as they caught each other up on all that had transpired since they'd been separated. "I love it here." Morag waxed nostalgic as she spun around in a circle and took in the massive great hall and its bustling activity. "Stuart might be a bit high-handed at times, but he's good to me, gentle with me. No' at all a tyrant as my damned brothers were."

Janet didn't know the first thing about Stuart, but she could agree with that bit about Morag's brothers. She shook her head, bemused. "Are you telling me you don't want to go back to the future?"

Morag sighed, then shrugged. "I really don't know, Janet. I was no' thrilled with my life back in Nairn, hated it in fact. I would have gone crazy had I no' had you for a friend."

"I know what you mean," Janet murmured, her cat-like green eyes straying to absently watch Glynna play dolls with her friend. "But I can't imagine life here will be easy either." Her brow wrinkled as she considered something. She glanced back toward Morag. "Do you even know where we will be living once we leave the castle? Are Euan and Stuart sort of like, I don't know, soldiers to the big guy here or something?"

Morag's mouth dropped open. "You mean you do no' know?"

"Know what?"

Morag chuckled. "Janet, lovie, Stuart is a soldier to the big guy, as you so aptly named him, but Euan *is* the big guy."

Janet's eyes blinked a few times in rapid succession. She wasn't exactly sure what Morag...oh my.

Janet's eyes strayed across the hall to where her husband was instructing a man to send a message from him to another laird. She couldn't eavesdrop on much of the conversation—they were standing too far apart—but she did manage to make out the last sentence he'd uttered. *Tell him Mac Dhonuill nan Eilean sent ye.*

Mac Dhonuill nan Eilean?

Janet's breath caught in the back of her throat. She swallowed roughly as her gaze darted back toward a grinning Morag.

"That's right," Morag nodded. "You married the MacDonald of the Isles."

Chapter Ten

Euan gazed down at the slumbering form of the woman sound asleep beside him. He'd loved her hard this eve, ridden her sweet cunt twice and her wanton mouth once before he'd felt sated enough to leave her be.

'Twas little wonder, he thought with more than a wee bit of male pride, that his lady wife was snoring louder than Auld Sheumais did when he'd been hitting the ale overlong. Of course, he conceded in a rare flash of amusement, her snoring was also making it difficult to fall asleep.

Reclining on his elbow, Euan ran his fingers through Janet's shiny mane of curls, brushing a few stray ones back from her hairline. 'Twas hard to believe that a woman so finely made was his. 'Twas not just her plump breasts and woman's hips that tempted him so, nor even the way she gave herself over to him so willingly.

'Twas her heart as well. The way she was with wee Glynna, taking to her these past few weeks as if she'd birthed her herself, spending time with her and making her feel important.

'Twas also the way Janet made him feel. When he held his wife in his arms and made love to her, or simply when his eyes clashed with hers from across a chamber, he felt…alive. Whole and content. 'Twas the first he'd felt this way in — well mayhap in forever.

Euan bent his neck to kiss Janet softly on the lips. He hadn't been expecting it, but was pleased when she woke up, blinked a couple of times as if coming out of a daze, then smiled slowly before pulling his face down atop hers to kiss him more thoroughly.

They kissed for a few minutes, softly moaning into each other's mouths as their tongues swept back and forth over the other's. After a bit more of this languid loving, Euan raised his dark head and gazed down into Janet's eyes. "Ye're awake," he murmured.

"Yes." She nibbled on her lip for a moment. "Plan to do anything about it?" she whispered, her cheeks tinting scarlet as the words tumbled out.

Euan couldn't help but to grin, something he found himself doing quite a bit of lately. And now that his wife understood his tongue almost as well as he did, he'd discovered much to his delight that she had a wondrous sense of humor. She never bored him. Never a dull moment at the keep with Janet about.

'Twas not her words that caused his grin this time, though, but the fact that her cheeks were pink. As many times and in as many ways as they'd loved each other, it never failed to amuse him when Janet would suddenly turn shy on him. "And what," he murmured, "would ye have me tae do aboot it, vixen?"

She grinned at his endearment, having never thought of herself in such outrageous terms before. Or at least not before meeting Euan. She'd been telling herself for weeks not to form a deeper attachment to him, not to let herself fall any more in love with him, until she knew with stark clarity just what it was that she wanted. Did she want to remain in the past or try to find her way back to the future?

But as usual where Euan was concerned, the moment he gazed into her eyes with longing she brushed her concerns aside and refused to deal with them. It was wrong, she knew, but she couldn't seem to help herself.

"Hmm," she teased, pretending to think his question over. "Perhaps you could read to me by the fire or—"

Euan half growled and half grinned as he came down on top of Janet and settled himself between her thighs. She giggled, running her hand along the strong line of his jaw. It was always good to see the proof of him feeling carefree and lighthearted. Since arriving, she'd quickly discovered that such common things were contrary to his nature, most likely borne of his position in life. From a young age, he had ruled many. Not only that but he'd been responsible for the rearing of his brothers as well.

He entered her welcoming flesh in one long thrust, gritting his teeth as he did so. 'Twas like a bit of heaven on earth, being deep inside of her. "I've got a treatise ye can ponder o'er, lass."

Janet's eyes widened on a laugh. She'd never heard him crack a joke before. He'd done it fairly well for a novice. "Oh do you now?" She grinned, wrapping her legs around his waist. "Anywhere near as good as *The Odyssey*?"

"Much better, I'm thinkin'." He rotated his hips and thrust deeply to underscore his words.

"I see," Janet gasped. "And what is the name of this treatise?"

Euan slid into her flesh again, causing his wife to suck in her breath. He ground his teeth, beads of perspiration forming on his brow. "I call it *Mac Dhonuill nan Eilean Falls In Love*."

Janet stilled. MacDonald of the Isles Falls In…Love? She had been expecting a witty return, not a declaration of his feelings. Her eyes darted up to meet his, rounding when she saw the affection in his gaze. She realized at once that her husband was deadly serious. *He loved her.*

"Oh, Euan," she whispered, "thank-you so much for telling me that." *It made her decision so much easier.*

He grunted a bit, hopelessly attempting to conceal the rising color in his cheeks. "Have ye nothing tae say back tae me, wife?" He glanced away, wishing he hadn't asked as much.

It dawned on Euan that for the first time in his life he was feeling quite vulnerable. He quickly decided he didn't care much for the feeling, but also realized there was naught to be done about it. "Forgive my tongue," he said gruffly, "I should no' have—"

"Euan," Janet murmured, clutching his face between her hands as she searched his eyes.

"Aye?"

She smiled. "I love you too."

The heat in his face went from pink to crimson, endearing him to his wife all the more. "Of course ye do," he grumbled under his breath. "Let us speak of these silly things no more, ye ken?"

She grinned. "But I really love those silly things."

He sighed like a martyr. "Did I know ye were tae be so bluidy demanding, I mayhap would no' have stolen ye, Janet mine."

She slapped him playfully on the rump for that. "Oh really?"

Euan grinned, then shook his head slightly as he studied her features with a serious expression. "That's no' the truth," he murmured. "I would have stolen ye no matter the circumstance."

"Why?" she whispered.

He kissed her softly on the lips. "Because I love ye." The dimple on his cheek popped out as he added teasingly, "daft wench."

Chapter Eleven

Lack of TV—not a problem. No electricity—who cares? Non-flushing latrines made of stone—kids' stuff.

Janet breezed around the keep for the next couple of days feeling drunk on giddiness. He loved her. Handsome, virile, sexy Euan was in love with mousy Janet Donald nee Duval.

So it was much to her chagrin when Morag squirreled her away in an alcove on the second day following Euan's pronouncement of love, wanting to escape.

"I can no' stand to be with Stuart, Janet." Morag threw a lock of red hair over her shoulder. "Did I say he's no' as bad as my brothers? Ha! He is a thousand times worse!"

Janet cleared her throat. "What did he do?"

"What didn't he do is more the question needing asked," Morag huffed. "He tells me what to do, orders me around like a bloody personal servant, he…"

Janet listened with half an ear as Morag detailed the longish litany of her husband's sins. She knew Morag— and her temper—well. Even though her best friend didn't realize how she got when she was in a pique, Janet understood implicitly that she'd change her mind about wanting to leave Stuart once she cooled down a bit. She knew Morag loved him. It's just that Morag always became agitated whenever a man displayed even a hint of behavior that smacked of her brothers'. A fact Janet could hardly blame her for.

"So are you with me or no'?" Morag finished her tirade with a definitive nod of the head. "Or do you plan to make me find passage back to Nairn myself?"

Three years of experience enabled Janet to deal with the potentially explosive situation pragmatically. She knew Morag would change her mind once she let off a bit more steam. It was just a matter of distracting her until then.

Janet pretended to turn the matter over a bit. She narrowed her eyes and gazed thoughtfully toward the ceiling. "I don't think we should discuss this here. Let's go take a walk outside," she whispered.

Morag's blue gaze rounded as if she hadn't expected Janet to capitulate in the slightest and, in fact, had been hoping she wouldn't. That only confirmed Janet's initial suspicion — Morag just wanted to vent. "Y-You want to discuss it outside?"

"Of course." Janet shrugged. "This is hardly the sort of thing we can talk about in here."

Morag was so taken aback it didn't occur to her that there was no reason they couldn't talk within the castle walls because nobody would understand them anyway. "Well…" She scrunched up her face and cocked her head. "You want to leave Euan?" she squeaked out.

Janet decided not to bother playing games. Clearly, Morag had no desire to leave. Not deep down inside at any rate. "Not any more than you want to leave Stuart." She held out her hand and smiled. "Come on. Why don't we go outside and take a nice brisk walk and you can tell me all about what a jerk he is and then you'll feel tons better and more ready to confront him."

Morag chuckled. "You know me too damn well, lovie."

"Lucky for you." Janet grinned. "If I was any other woman we would have been half way to Nairn by now."

* * * * *

"I dinna ken her problem," Stuart growled, his sword clashing against Euan's. They were sparring in the lower bailey, honing their skills.

Euan disarmed him almost immediately, then pointed the tip of his sword just under his brother's chin. "Ye best figure it out, mon. 'Tis affecting your concentration." He released him and sheathed his weapon.

Graeme, who had been watching from the sidelines, chose that moment to amble over and do a little grumbling of his own. "At least ye have a wench tae moan o'er, Stuart. I still can no' believe Auld Sheumais let wee Elizabeth get away from him." He threw his hands in the air dramatically. "All the mon had tae do was watch her whilst I took a piss!"

Stuart found a grin at that. "He'd been hitting the cups again, no doubt."

Euan snorted. "As always." He shook his head, then rumpled Graeme's hair affectionately. "'Tis tae young ye are tae worry o'er a wench, boy. Ye'll get another. I'll find ye a betrothed myself come Michaelmas when a few of the clan leaders come tae sup."

Graeme shivered at the notion. "I can scarcely contain my excitement, brother. Will ye betroth me tae that MacPherson wench who possesses a face with a frighteningly close resemblance tae that of a pig, or will it be the dowered daughter of the MacInnis with the overlarge teeth?"

Euan and Stuart couldn't help but to chuckle. "Well," Stuart teased, "what is your preference? A pig face or overlarge teeth?"

Graeme didn't see the humor in the situation. He sniffed at such a choice. "Ye best save your ill-wit for one who can appreciate it. Since I dinna care for it and since your lady wife is planning tae run away from ye, one must wonder—"

"Back up, whelp," Stuart interrupted. His smile faded abruptly. "What do ye mean Morag plans tae run away?"

Graeme's eyes widened. "Well," he stammered out, "she was mayhap no' serious. Mayhap she was just grumblin' aboot because she was mad at—"

"Graeme," Stuart ground out, "tell me what ye heard."

"Aye," Euan rumbled, his thoughts turning to Janet and her close friendship with Stuart's wife. "Tell us."

Graeme sighed, thinking the scene he'd witnessed this morn not worth the telling of it, but eventually he gave in with a shrug. Why not? "I dinna ken most of what she said for she was mutterin' tae herself in that foreign tongue of hers, but after ye stomped off from the great hall this morn she grumbled under her breath in Gaelic that she was off tae find Janet and leave this place forever."

A chill of foreboding coursed down Euan's spine. Janet had never even confessed to him from whence she'd come. If she got away, he wouldn't have the foggiest notion where to hunt her down.

"Damme!" Angered, Stuart cursed up a mild storm before turning back to his brothers. "I best go see what the wench is aboot."

"I'll come with ye," Euan murmured.

Stuart's eyes rounded comprehendingly. He nodded. "Let us go."

Chapter Twelve

Morag twirled a freshly picked bluebell between her fingers and smiled as the women walked alongside the perimeter of the wall that led toward the waters surrounding Skye. "You were right," she admitted on a grin, "I feel a lot better now. Sunshine and sea breeze was just the thing."

Janet tossed a tawny ringlet over her shoulder and smiled. "It is quite beautiful here, isn't it?"

"Mmm. Like a dream."

Janet stopped when they came toward an area of the wall with a hole in it. Gliding up to it, she put her eye against it and looked to what was beyond the stone structure. "Wow. Morag come look at this. The beach out there is about the prettiest thing I've ever seen."

Morag tried to oblige her, but wasn't able to see anything. "I'm shorter than you by a good three inches and you are standing on tiptoe. I canna see a blessed thing."

Janet chuckled. "Too bad. It's so pretty."

Morag thought that over for a second as she surveyed the wall. "We could try to climb to the top using these holes as toeholds."

Janet wrinkled her nose at that. "What if we fall? No thanks!"

Morag sighed. "Janet, we may love our husbands but let's face it, there is no' a damn thing to do in this time. If we fall, so what. At least trying to climb the wall gives us something to do for the next fifteen minutes!"

Janet half laughed and half snorted. "True."

Five minutes later the women had gotten no more than halfway up the wall when the thundering sound of horses' hooves came rumbling from the castle bailey charging toward them at top speed.

Morag crinkled up her face, glancing over her shoulder without letting go of her hold on the wall. "Is that my Stuart?"

Janet used one hand to shield her eyes from the sun's glare. "Yep. And that looks like Euan with him too." She winced when she heard Stuart's cursing. "Wonder what's got him so upset?"

Morag's eyes widened. "You do no' suppose we are under attack?"

Janet wasn't given the opportunity to answer. Twenty mounted men came to an abrupt halt at the wall just then, all of them staring straight up at the women from below ground. They looked distinctly uncomfortable, Janet thought, which seemed a bit odd. But then again, Stuart was cursing loud enough to wake the dead. That would make anybody uncomfortable.

"What are you bellowing over now?" Morag screeched, her nostrils flaring as she glanced defiantly down toward her husband.

Stuart didn't answer that. He didn't bother. Janet thought his face looked red enough to start a campfire off of. "Get," he said distinctly, spacing out his words evenly, "down from there now."

Morag chose that moment to contradict him. "No," she sniffed. "I will no'."

A tic began to work in Stuart's jaw, which Janet found curious. He really seemed to be overreacting to the situation if indeed she and Morag's excursion up the wall was what had set him off.

"Morag!" he bellowed. "Running away will do ye no' a bit of good. I will find ye every time. And punish ye just as I will when I get my hands on ye!"

Morag rolled her eyes. "Oh sure, like I'll come down now," she said dryly, "knowin' you plan to punish me and all." She sighed. "I mean really Stuart, you—" She broke off as she glanced toward Janet. Confused, she threw her a baffled look before doing the same to her husband. "Wait one moment. What do you mean aboot running away, Stuart? I was no' running away. We were but climbing the wall to get a look at the beach on the other side."

A few muffled laughs rose up from the soldiers on horseback, inducing Janet to wince. Geez but she couldn't blame them. She knew for a fact Morag was telling the truth, but climbing a wall to look at the beach? It truly did sound like a lie, and a weak one at that.

"Climbing a wall tae look at the bluidy beach?" Stuart laughed mirthlessly. "How lack-witted do ye think I am, woman?"

When Morag opened her mouth to speak, Janet forestalled her by coming to her defense. She was afraid that, as angry as her best friend was, she might have chosen to actually answer Stuart's question, thereby getting herself into hotter waters with him. "It's the truth," she said with a nod, gazing down at her brother-in-law.

"She wasn't running away. We were just bored and we wanted to—"

"Enough."

That one word, uttered quietly yet icily from Euan was enough to send a shiver up Janet's spine. She flicked her gaze down toward her husband, swallowing roughly when she realized how angry he was. But there was more than anger in his expression. There was something else. Something that looked remarkably like...pain.

Oh no! she thought in a flash of realization, Euan actually believed that Morag had been trying to run away. And worse yet, Janet now understood that he believed her to be guilty of the same crime. Her eyes rounding, she implored her husband to listen. "You don't really think I was trying to run from you do you?"

He said nothing. Merely stared at her.

"Do you?" she asked shrilly.

Euan was wearing his mask again, Janet noted with more than a little trepidation. His black gaze was boring holes into her, the line of his jaw stubborn and unbending. Her eyes widened nervously.

After what felt like an eternity, Euan broke his harsh gaze from hers and threw a command at one of his men. "Get her down from there," he said with seeming indifference. "And lock her in my bedchamber."

Chapter Thirteen

Janet's cheeks pinkened with mingled anger and embarrassment as Euan's man Niall escorted her back to her sleeping chamber. Her only consolation was that the gruff warrior looked as though he felt sorry for her. In fact, just before he locked her inside he turned to her and mumbled sheepishly, "For the record, milady, I do no' think ye were tryin' tae escape."

And then he was gone, leaving Janet alone to stew. She was angry. Very angry. But also quite frightened. The final look Euan had thrown her way before galloping off had been laced with promises of retribution. She could only wonder at his punishment.

One side of her, the indignant half, wanted to stay right where she was and await his arrival so she could rage at him for treating her like this, for not believing her when she'd told him the truth. But the other side of her, the pragmatic half, wanted to bolt. Janet had no clue as to how her husband planned to punish her for her alleged sin, but she conceded rather gloomily that none of the scenarios she was coming up with in her mind boded well.

Janet paced back and forth in the bedchamber, uncertain as to what she should do, what she should say, when Euan finally saw fit to make an appearance. Just then the door came crashing open, causing Janet to whirl around on her heel and her gaze to dart nervously toward her husband.

He looked angry. Very, very angry. For some reason or another she wasn't afraid of him any longer though. For some reason or another rather than cowering as most would have and she probably should have, she found her eyes narrowing acidly and her lips pinching together. "Go away," she seethed, turning around, giving him her back. "I have nothing to say to you."

It took Euan five long strides to reach her. When he did, he whirled her around to face him. "I'm certain ye are verra angry with me," he gritted out, his nostrils flaring, "for putting a stop tae your grand plan. But ye will do as I bid ye regardless."

That was too much. She thumped him on a steely arm, not that the big ogre so much as flinched from it. "This is ridiculous!" she screeched, raising her voice to him for the first time since they'd met. "I wasn't trying to run," she fumed, "and I resent the fact that you don't believe me!"

His nostrils were still flaring as he searched her gaze. He looked like he wanted to believe her but was afraid to hope. And then the vulnerability in his eyes was quickly masked and the steel replaced it. "Take your clothes off," he ordered her.

Janet's eyes widened. Her chin went up a notch. "No."

"I said," Euan repeated icily, "take your clothes off." A tic was working in his cheek now.

"I heard you and I said no." She crossed her arms defiantly over her breasts.

Apparently he didn't care for that answer for the next thing Janet knew he was lifting up her skirt and removing her dress himself. She struggled, indignant now. "How dare you!" she sputtered as the dress went over her head and sailed towards the other side of the room.

"I am Euan Donald, Mac Dhonuill nan Eilean," he said arrogantly. "I dare what I will." His black gaze raked her body insolently. "Go lie on the bed."

"Are you deaf?" she screeched. "I don't wish to speak to you let alone have sex with you! You didn't believe me when I told you the truth and I have nothing more to say to you!"

A vein in his neck began to pulse as his face stained red with anger. "Ye expect me tae believe ye were climbing up the wall tae see the beach!" he roared.

"Yes! I expect you to believe it!"

Euan growled like a trapped animal, the need to believe his wife warring with rational thought. He didn't know what to think in that moment, just knew that he needed to be inside of her. *"Get on the bed,"* he bellowed.

Her chin lifted impossibly higher. "No!"

He slashed his hand through the air. *"Now."*

Janet's eyes widened at the unadulterated pain laced in that one word. It was that knowledge, and not the order itself, that sent her legs gliding toward the bed. Climbing up on top of it, she sat there on her knees and waited, uncertain as to how she could convince him she had been telling the truth out there on the wall. It was paramount that she convince him. She didn't want him hurting inside.

"Why did ye run?" he asked as he took off his clothing and joined her on the raised bed. "Did ye really think I'd let ye go?" He ground that question out through clenched jaws as he came down on his knees in front of her and took her breasts in his palms. "Ye should have known better, *Seonaidh, leamsa.*" *Janet, mine.*

She met his tortured look unflinchingly. "I did not run from you."

His black gaze softened somewhat, but Janet could tell he wasn't yet totally convinced. He was beginning to believe her, though, which gave her new hope.

And then Euan was massaging her nipples, rubbing them between his thumbs and forefingers and Janet found her lips parting on a breathy sigh under the sensual assault. "Ye have beautiful thick nipples," he said gruffly as he plumped them. "I want them pokin' straight up in the sky for me tae suckle of."

Janet gasped as his lips closed around one diamond-hard nipple. He slurped it into his mouth, closing his eyes as if to savor it, rolling it around between his tongue and teeth. Liquid desire shot through her, dampening the flesh between her legs and elongating her nipples further. She ran her fingers through his hair and mashed his face into her chest. "Yes, Euan," she breathed out. "Oh yes."

He drew from her hard then, sucking on her nipples incessantly until she was panting for air and he was primal with the need to fill her up with his cock and his cum.

"Whether ye want me or no'," Euan rasped out in a moment of unveiled vulnerability, as he pushed her down onto her back and settled himself between her thighs, "I will always want ye. I will always need ye."

Janet's eyes closed briefly, saddened as she was by the pain in his voice. Her eyes opened and clashed with his. "I love you, Euan. I swear to you," she promised softly, "that as ludicrous as my explanation might have sounded back there at the wall, it was the complete and total truth." She wrapped her legs around his waist. "I will never run from you. I love you."

He lay poised above her, his eyes searching hers frantically for the truth, hoping against hope that he could believe what he'd been told.

"Tha gaol agam ort, a Euan." *I love you, Euan.*

He impaled her in one long stroke, inducing Janet to gasp as he filled her. "I love ye tae," he rasped out, his teeth gritting at the exquisite feel of her tight flesh enveloping him, sucking him in.

Janet clutched his buttocks in her hands and stroked them soothingly. "Do you believe me then?" she whispered. "Please tell me you do. Even if it's a lie. I couldn't bear it if I thought you believed Stuart."

Euan kissed her lips gently, sipping at them. "I believe ye, my love. And that's no' a lie."

Janet had no time to respond to that pronouncement, for within the next breath her legs had been thrown over his shoulders and Euan was drawing himself up to his knees. His callused fingers digging into the flesh of her hips, he held her steady and impaled her to the hilt.

"Oh yes."

"Mmm," he said thickly as he began to rock in and out of her cunt in long, deep strokes, "ye feel so good tae me." He thrust harder and deeper, his strokes becoming faster and more penetrating.

"Oh god."

The sound of her vagina sucking up Euan's steely flesh was as much of a turn-on to Janet as her husband's primal pumping. She bore down on his cock, meeting his thrusts, loving the deep mounting he gave to her when her legs were splayed wide over his shoulders. *"Faster."*

Euan's jaw clenched tightly, his muscles cording and tensing, the veins on his neck and arms bulging. Grabbing her thighs, he pounded into her slick flesh.

Faster. Harder. Faster still.

"Oh yes."

And then Janet was coming, her back arching and her head falling back in ecstasy as she moaned wantonly for him, her nipples stabbing upwards as her sopping flesh contracted around the length and breadth of him. "*Yeeeeessssss,*" she groaned, gyrating her hips at him as her cunt sucked every bit of pleasure from him that she could.

"*Janet.*" Euan used his fingers to clamp down on her jutting nipples as he thrust into her once, twice, three times more. Throwing his head back, he made a guttural sound as his orgasm ripped through him, spewing into her flesh.

Both of them dripping in perspiration, Euan held his body over Janet's while they both steadied their breathing. He kissed her softly on the lips, then eased her splayed legs from off of his shoulders. Coming down on the bed beside her, he drew her into his arms. "I love ye," he murmured, kissing her temple.

She smiled contentedly. "I love you too."

They were silent for a long while, enjoying the simple pleasure of basking in each other's embrace. Eventually it was Euan who broke the languid quiet. "I was wondering aboot something," he said, stroking her thigh as he spoke.

"Mmm. What about?"

"Ye are no' of the clan Hay."

Janet grinned, sensing the question that was coming. "No I'm not."

"Where did ye come from then?"

"It's a long story."

"We've plenty of time."

She smiled up at him, running her hand across the impressive width of his chest. "True. But before I tell you that story, I have something else I'd like to tell you first."

Euan cocked a black eyebrow. "Sounds intriguing. And ye sound mischievous. Should I round up a tankard of ale before we talk?"

She grinned. "You might need two."

Epilogue

Euan Donald, Lord of the Isles, master of all he surveyed, swiped an unmanly tear from his eye as he watched his beautiful wee Janet suckle their hour-old son Alistair. Bonny Glynna was sitting next to them on the bed, grinning down at her new baby brother as she held on to one of his tiny hands.

He thought back on that eve several months past when first his wife had told him she was carrying his bairn. She had been right, he thought with a grin, he had needed more than one tankard of ale. Though not from the announcement of his son's conception but from the tale of how Janet had come to be with him in the first place.

Odd, but Euan had believed every word, having decided after that day at the wall to never doubt his wife again. He wasn't a man given to trusting others, yet Janet he trusted both implicitly and explicitly. 'Twas a good feeling, having another in the world he knew he could always rely upon.

"Look, Da'," Glynna giggled, "he's all red and wrinkly."

Janet laughed. "I'm sure he'll grow out of it, sweetheart."

Euan grinned at his wife and daughter as he strode toward the bed to join his family. "Let's hope so. Otherwise he might no' be verra popular with the ladies."

Janet and Glynna giggled at that, warming his heart.

It occurred to Euan as he sat down and gathered his wife and children closer to him that a year ago when he'd first set out to steal a bride, he had never anticipated finding such bliss. Fate was a funny thing.

Thank the saints.

The Seduction of Sean Nolan
by Treva Harte

Chapter One

He was dying. The heat inside him felt like he was still in the thick of battle, with the sun beating down and the cannons shaking the parched earth.

He was thirsty. Just as thirsty as he'd been during the fighting near Manassas. Now fever was burning him up.

There still wasn't any water. He knew not to expect any by now. He'd yelled for water at first, but no one had come. At first he'd been shoved into an isolated corner of the warehouse they called a field hospital. After a few days he'd been carted off to this place and dumped in another corner. Once again, he'd been forgotten and left to die.

Maybe it was just as well. He knew they'd take off his leg if they saw him. He'd heard the screams of the other men. He'd seen them carried out, off of the surgeon's table. He'd seen them carted away days later, dead. Not many survived the surgery.

He had only one real regret. His wasn't any of the ones he'd heard others moaning out loud. He didn't have any family left, so he didn't have to be sorry about leaving anyone. He'd done what he was supposed to do as a soldier and he wasn't ashamed of doing his duty, but he wouldn't regret not being one anymore, either. He'd been sixteen when he'd agreed to join up for the hundred-dollar bonus. He didn't regret that. That extra money had allowed his ma to be cared for in comfort before she died. He'd have enlisted sometime for the money anyway. Poor men did.

No, his only regret was that he had grown into a man, but now he'd never have a chance to be one. He hadn't wanted his first time to be with a whore. His life hadn't allowed him to be with any other kind of woman.

Lord, he didn't want to die a virgin.

"God, maybe a woman of pleasure isn't what I should pray for, but I'm asking for that regardless." He mouthed the supplication, unable to say the words out loud. His throat was too dry.

To escape the pain, the screams, the smells and the thirst, he drifted back into a half-sleep.

* * * * *

Nell sat in front of her computer, rubbing her forehead and sipping on some iced tea. It was hot out there. Even with the window air conditioner unit up full-blast, the room was scorching.

Of course the air conditioning unit could be out. She made a face. She couldn't afford to pay a repairman right now. One reason the place was cheap was because you had to provide your own cooling unit. That had seemed all right earlier in the year when it was cool. She'd decided a small, cheap unit would work just fine.

Now it was late summer and, once again, she'd budgeted badly. She should have bought a bigger unit before summer when the prices for air conditioning units had gone up. But it was hard to budget when you didn't have any money. Being a teaching assistant never paid well and her determination to write in the summer instead of teaching as many college classes as she could was taking its toll on her bank account.

But she had been desperate to work on her history of the area this summer. Publish or perish. She'd even moved to Manassas to research her subject up close. Nell was getting close enough to her doctorate to think about the job interviews next year. She needed a good scholarly article to point to on her resume. She needed to finish her dissertation. The combination of teaching and a fellowship paid the bills — barely.

The future was the problem. If she didn't write something publishable soon she'd never have a shot at really teaching and researching as a professor. Her parents would have been right all along when they'd refused to help finance her education, telling her she could waste her time but not their money.

Maybe they were right, but she loved history. All she'd ever really wanted to do was to research and write and bring history alive.

Not that Nell could muster up much enthusiasm to write at the moment. It was so hot. Hot outside, boring and futile inside. She was never going to get this article on local Civil War battles done. She was concentrating on the second Battle of Manassas, the one most people ignored. She felt like ignoring it right now herself.

Nell held the glass to her forehead and then her chest, feeling the condensation drip against her skin. That felt good. She might as well enjoy the cool sensation tickling its way down between her breasts. Nothing else would get done today. She knew she wasn't able to write any longer. It was too damn miserable to think. She was just going to close her eyes and...

* * * * *

His prayers had been answered. Not in any way he'd expected. The woman in front of him didn't look quite real. She didn't look like a whore either. He wondered if he had died and this was a ghost or an angel. But she felt real enough when she pressed her hand up against his lips.

She felt real and cool to the touch.

"Well, you're alive and breathing here. Wherever here is. But you're not alive by much," he heard her say. "This hospital can't be what it looks like it is—my God. What an awful place."

"Yes, ma'am," he whispered.

Her hand touched his face again and he shut his eyes. He could smell perfume and clean skin. Her touch was soft and gentle against his feverish skin. Everything about this dream-woman felt good.

He opened his eyes again. She might feel good, but she looked a little odd. Her brown hair was cut shorter than he'd ever seen a woman's cut before and she was wearing some baggy things that looked almost like short pants. Women didn't wear pants, so they couldn't be. Her shirt was tight against her body and he could see her breasts. High, pear-shaped breasts that looked like they could fit in his hand. He could see long, white legs.

In fact, now that he thought about it, she didn't look odd. She looked perfect.

"You're in bad shape, mister. But I guess you know that."

"Yes'm," he croaked out between parched lips. "Water?"

"You're thirsty, too. Of course. And there isn't any to be had that I can see." She sighed. "I suppose any water that is around here is crawling with bugs."

"Yes'm. Most likely." It hurt to talk, but he wanted her to stay with him. If they talked, she wouldn't vanish.

She looked down and hissed.

"I don't believe this. I have my glass. I wish I hadn't drunk all the tea, but at least I brought along some ice. I hope it won't make you sick. I suppose you can't feel much sicker than you are now — "

His eyes had shut after the effort of talking. He tried to concentrate on what she was saying but the words swirled around him, sometimes clear, sometimes not. Then he felt something cold and wet on his tongue.

Frozen water. Ice melting against the heat in his mouth.

She was an angel. She had to be. No one else could conjure up ice in this hell.

He let it slide against his tongue and puddle away.

"Try just one ice chip," she gently whispered. "We'll see how that goes. If that works, we can try another."

He opened his mouth and moved his head, blindly looking for more.

"Soon. I promise. There's more."

Her hand stroked him again. Her voice sounded odd, but the ice and the hand felt just right.

The second time she gave him ice, her arm slid under his head and she leaned closer to put the chip against his mouth. He felt her fingers against his lips. Then he felt her breasts up against his chest.

Thank you, Lord. That might not be all he wanted, but that might be all he could handle for now.

If she stayed, he'd be willing to live a little longer.

"Were you hurt anywhere but your leg?"

"No'm. Got a fever, though."

"Let's hope it's nothing contagious. By the way, my name is Nell. Eleanor, actually. But call me Nell."

"Nell."

"And you? Since we're getting so cozy here, don't you think you could tell me your name?"

"Nolan."

He felt her hands undoing the button at his waistband. His breath caught when he felt her fingers probing the pants fly.

"How do these things come undone anyhow?"

Her fingers found the covered panel at last. She tugged at the first button.

"This is harder than it looks."

He believed her.

One button, two, three, the fourth… Then she began to push the pants down.

Oh, yes. Thank you, Lord. He was feeling weak as a baby, but if the Lord was providing this then maybe the Lord would give him the strength to do what he'd been wanting to do, to grant him his one last wish.

"What's with these underpants? How does anyone get out of these things?" She unbuttoned the fastening halfway down his muslin drawers.

He still couldn't open his eyes, but he could feel his penis stiffening. No. He wasn't dead. With his pants opened, he knew she could see what was happening to him. He couldn't hide his arousal.

"That's an ugly wound. It needs a doctor."

"Don't want one of the doctors here." He managed to say it out loud.

Her hand brushed near his thigh.

"Whoa, Nolan. Maybe you aren't as sick as I thought." He could hear the smile in her voice, but he didn't want to smile.

He swallowed.

"Please." He wasn't able to say more.

She gave him more ice. That was good, but not what he wanted now. He could feel himself getting harder as she ran a finger against his leg. The wound was throbbing some, though not as bad as it had been. Something else was starting to hurt now.

"You're stronger than you look, Nolan. But you probably shouldn't even try what it is you want to try."

"Nell. *Please.*"

He'd probably offended his angel. Maybe angels didn't do such things. But if there was any chance she would, he had to ask.

"Nell, likely I'm gonna die soon. Please." He could feel sweat forming. "I want this more'n anything. I've never had anything like this before."

He was going to lose her.

The silence was long and, even while he knew she was angry and going to leave, he felt his erection getting harder yet.

Maybe she wouldn't leave. After all, she was still here now. Maybe she'd have mercy on him before she left.

Nell hesitated.

His silent desperation was making her feel surprisingly responsive. She could feel just the beginnings of a sexual ache start in her. Nell had only admitted this to herself, but she'd always fantasized about Civil War soldiers.

Of course it didn't hurt that this one was young and stared at her as if she was some kind of goddess. Or that he had an amazingly large cock. She wondered how responsive that cock would be.

Then again, he was filthy. And then again, none of this could be real. Why not make this un-real man who was so ready for her happy? Why not make herself happy? She hadn't been with a man in a long time and she missed the feel of it.

"I—Here." Her hand was soft but stronger than he'd thought.

When her fingers first grasped his shaft, he opened his eyes. Then he gasped. Her hands were over him, stroking him harder and then harder yet. He watched her fingers tickling at the head of his penis and his erection jerked.

He hadn't ever thought of this. He hadn't known to think of this.

"I'll be gentle, Nolan. I don't want to hurt you."

"Do whatever—you want. Nell." He managed to say it through surges of intense pleasure.

This would be a good way to die. The hospital was dark. It was night. No one would see them here. If he could just stay quiet so no one would come—

"You're so beautiful." He gasped the words, feeling dizzy.

That should be enough. He knew her touch ought to be, but he couldn't help himself. He didn't even know why he did it, but he reached out to grab her hair and pull her closer.

He felt her hesitate again.

Then he felt a mouth cover him and wrap around his penis. He'd never thought of this before either, never knew a woman would put her mouth *there*.

The first touch was soft. That didn't matter. Her mouth felt so good. He moaned, then threw a hand over his mouth and bit into his fingers. No one must hear. No one must show up and stop her —

He felt her tongue stroking where her fingers had been before. Every time he thought no sensation could be better than the one she just sent through him, she found something better yet to do to him. He began to shudder.

He tried to force himself to wait, to withdraw. If he was going to die now, he wanted the last pleasure he had on earth to last longer than this.

But Nell's mouth had turned from soft to greedy. He could hear the sucking sounds it made and he moaned again against his hand. He shuddered harder and still he forced himself to wait. Then her fingers began to work in partnership with her mouth. He felt the stroking against his scrotum and he knew he couldn't last anymore.

This might not be exactly what he'd wanted, but it was plenty good enough. Still, he tried to protest. He took the hand from his mouth.

"But I want you. I want to be in you!" He knew it was too late.

He groaned loudly, fingers gripping into the straw that made up his hospital bed as he spurted hard into her mouth.

Nell's mouth and fingers were relentless, milking him. He'd used his own hand a time or two before even though he'd known it wasn't right, but his hand had never felt like this...

He was shaking all over with his climax. His release almost hurt, it felt so good. He gasped in his throat, and felt blackness rushing up.

No. Not yet. *Not yet.*

He wanted more. He'd been wrong, Lord. This wasn't enough.

More!

"You stay with me, Nolan. Damn, don't you keel over now!"

He heard her voice.

"Stay with me. Do you hear?"

He wanted more than anything to obey her.

Then he felt and saw nothing.

Chapter Two

Nell's head hurt when she woke up, staring at the now black computer screen. It was still hot, but after her dream, the room didn't seem nearly as bad as it had.

She looked at the high ceilings with sudden affection. This place was funky; it hadn't been fixed up properly since it had been built a hundred years ago, but at the moment home looked really good.

She jarred the computer's mouse and the screen blinked back on, back to the spot where she'd drifted off. She stared at the words in front of her. Maybe it hadn't been surprising that she'd dreamed about a hospital. A hospital that was in the Capitol building during the Civil War. She had been writing a paragraph about that in her article.

The wounded were brought to the Capitol to be tended to, to live or die as God disposed. Since the nursing was at best unskilled and the surgery was performed under less than hygienic conditions, it wasn't surprising that the men who fell at Manassas died like flies in the hospitals. Being nursed in the nation's Capitol made no difference in the quality of their care.

"Poor Nolan." She whispered out loud.

All she'd had to give him was a glass of ice. Melting ice at that. He'd been so sick, half-delirious with fever and pain. Then she'd...

Even though it had been a dream, she blushed.

He'd been sick, unshaven, and gaunt. But he'd held the promise of being beautiful. If he'd filled out and been healthy he would have been breathtaking. A real fantasy man. He hadn't looked bad even in his condition.

Piercing blue eyes that scorched her when he opened them. Red-gold hair. And certain parts of his body didn't need to fill out at all. She blushed again.

That had been quite a fantasy. She wondered how old her fantasy man had been. His raspy voice had sounded old, but what he had said made him sound young. Of course there were men who were virgins. Everyone had been one once. Maybe during the Civil War era men had been older before they'd had a woman. But she had a feeling he was younger than he'd looked.

What was she doing, seducing poor wounded boys almost half her age? Even in her dreams she didn't give blowjobs to guys she didn't even have a first name for. She could understand fantasizing about Union soldiers, since she was always reading so much about them, and heaven knows in this quiet little town there weren't many flesh-and-blood males to actually do anything with, but even so...

Nell could feel herself getting warmer and then, even more embarrassingly, getting wet. Giving herself a lecture on her fantasies wasn't doing any good. She was thinking about what she'd done in them. She was thinking about what Nolan had done in them. She was thinking about how grateful he'd been.

God, she needed to get a life.

And where was a real male to give her a hand when she needed one? she thought with a shake of her head. She hadn't been with one in far too long. Nell squirmed in her chair. If one of them helped her, she'd be as grateful as Nolan had been too.

She heard a sigh.

Nell knew she hadn't made that sigh, though she'd felt like heaving one. She looked over toward the threadbare couch and gasped.

Her fantasy man, huddled painfully on the too-short space available, was lying there. All too real blood was staining the cushions of the seats.

"I don't believe it." She whispered the words to herself.

Stay with me.

She'd said that to him. She'd meant him to stay conscious, to stay alive.

But he had done more. He had stayed with her outside of her dream.

He was truly flesh and blood. He had less blood with each passing moment, but he was flesh and blood all the same.

"What am I going to do?" Nell whispered it aloud, standing up so fast that her head spun for a moment.

Whatever he needed, he needed it fast.

* * * * *

"You're crazy, Nell." Kate grumbled the words to her as she bandaged the leg carefully. "If this leg gets worse, you're taking him to the hospital and you never, ever saw me do anything for him." She glanced at Nell pointedly. "Nothing at all."

"No hospital." Nell knew Nolan wouldn't be able to survive any more hospitals, not even a modern one. Especially not a modern one. "Listen, I don't know this guy but I'm sure he isn't the type to have insurance."

"He looks like he could be homeless," Kate agreed as she snapped her medical bag shut. "You don't know anything about him?"

"He says he's Nolan. From the looks of him, I guess he's a Civil War re-enactor. Some of them must be going way overboard for authenticity."

Nell didn't know if anyone would ever believe the story she'd concocted on the spur of the moment, but the latest anniversary and re-enactment of the Battle of Manassas had taken place a day or two ago. Besides, what other rational explanation was there to give? "He passed out before I got any more information."

"You history nuts get nuttier by the year." Kate shook her head.

Nell was just grateful that Kate was an emergency room technician and a good friend. "Please don't report him. As soon as he feels better, I'm sure he'll clear everything up."

"I'm not about to put my job in jeopardy over him," Kate told her. "I know I owe you a huge favor for introducing me to Marcos, but I think I've paid it back with this."

"You have. Thanks, Kate." Nell sensed Nolan was coming to, and she almost shoved her friend out the door. "I promise I'll keep an eye on him."

"Call me if you have problems with him." Kate left, but looked worried. "He looks like trouble to me."

"I will."

The antibiotics she'd bought but had neglected to take after her root canal would have to do. She shook one into her hand, frowning. She hoped this would do the trick. There was no way to get another prescription. Nell didn't know any doctors who would cater to her secrecy.

Her fantasy man opened his eyes and grunted when she pushed a pill in his mouth and then washed it down with water. He felt hotter to the touch and he'd felt plenty hot before.

"You're not going to die on me, are you?" Nell didn't want to think about how she'd ever explain that.

"I ain't dead?"

"No."

He looked around, as if trying to puzzle out what this place might be, and then his eyes shut again. Nell licked her lips. His clothes were filthy. She didn't like her couch much, but now that he'd lain there she had the feeling she could never sit on it again. She wondered what little creatures he'd brought with him from the nineteenth century.

No.

No, that wasn't right. Not the real nineteenth century.

That couldn't be right.

But when she unbuttoned his blue jacket, it felt authentic. No re-enactor, she thought as she nibbled on her lip, could come up with the smell of months of campfire smoke, unwashed sweat and blood. She eased it off of his body.

There were welts on his skin—maybe from battle, maybe from branches, maybe from bugs. She didn't want to think about it too closely. She threw the jacket into a plastic trash bag. Then she did the same to the long muslin shirt. The long, filthy muslin shirt.

Next the pants.

She licked her lips again. She remembered what had happened the last time she had done that. She ought to be better at getting them off on the second attempt.

But he was unconscious this time. He was sick and unconscious and—she couldn't help herself. She stroked the inside of his thighs as she gently took the pants off of him.

He responded again. She watched his erection slowly stiffen, fascinated with the sight.

He had to be young. Who else but a young man could do that when he should be half-dead? He opened his eyes, looking groggy, with spots of color on his white cheeks.

"Nell? You're here?"

"Oh...yes."

"What're you going to do with me now?"

She bit back telling him her first thoughts.

"Can you stand up, Nolan? First we're going to get you into the shower to get the dirt off. Then I believe I'm going to bathe you."

"Ain't had a bath in months," he muttered. "Maybe longer."

"I can tell." She braced herself yet still staggered when he pushed himself up.

He was tall for a Civil War soldier—maybe an inch or two under six feet. And he was heavier than she'd expected. They moved clumsily into the bathroom together.

For the first time Nell regretted the clawfoot tub in the bathroom. It would make all this very inconvenient.

"Swing your good leg in, Nolan."

His eyes half-closed, his erection still there, he obeyed her. She shoved at him and somehow got the rest of him in the tub. Then she turned on the showerhead.

He swayed, uncertainly, almost ready to fall.

"Oh, damn." She scrambled in to grab him. When he seemed able to stand on his own, though still swaying a little, Nell stripped herself of her clothing and threw it out of the tub.

She held him against her body as she began to lather his hair and torso. She took her time, making certain he was clean. And then —

She hesitated only once. She knew bugs hid in pubic hair.

She moved her hand forward. She also knew she wanted to touch. She began to massage in the soapsuds against, around, under his penis. She stroked the hair around the most sensitive areas.

He groaned.

He reached out to hold himself up against her even closer. Most of him might be weak, but there was one part of him that was still feeling strong.

She really ought not to do this to the poor fellow.

Of course she needed to. For his health. It was getting rid of any potential lice, she told herself.

She could feel her nipples hardening under the spray of the shower and against the abrasion of his chest hair.

This was for him. Right? Right.

"Nell, you're killing me all over again," she heard him groan against the top of her hair. His breath tickled her.

"I'm sorry," she murmured. Nell hesitated. Should she keep going?

"Don't stop." His voice was amused. "I'm getting used to it. Almost."

So she didn't. She was pleased to hear that the next sound that came out of his throat didn't sound amused at all. After all, she wasn't going to have him laughing at her when she was standing there, wet and naked and aroused, feeling him up. His growl was more what she had in mind.

"You know, it's not fair..." she whispered back to him.

"What?"

Her hand stilled. "You haven't touched me."

She could hear him swallow.

A suspended moment passed and then, finally, one large hand tentatively rested on her breast and then slid ever so slowly to her nipple. It tightened against his fingertips.

"I don't know what to do." He sounded embarrassed but interested.

"You have good instincts then." Nell knew she was the one who was amused now. "See where they take you."

He rolled the nipple between his fingers, his eyes glittering with fascination at the sight of it. His breathing grew labored as he watched it harden, watched her breath suck in and come in short gasps.

She was stunned when, without any more preliminaries, he slid down to his knees with an appreciative groan and moved his mouth against her pubic hair. She could feel his breath against her and she knew she was melting.

There was moisture everywhere. The shower rained down on her. She let her own wetness drip onto Nolan. Nolan's mouth and tongue were wet on her.

"*Ohh.*" Nell heard herself moan. She'd been so ready for him, so aroused with touching him, so aroused with the feel of his hand plucking her nipples, that she could feel herself rip into an orgasm almost immediately. By the time the sensation had passed, she was the one who felt unsteady. Unsteady, but still craving more.

She gripped his red-gold head, then moved her legs around his shoulders and rested her back against the wall. This had to be a fantasy, her fantasy, because he knew what to do, where to flick his tongue, where to suck— noisily—against her. "*Oh, God.*"

When she couldn't stand up anymore, she slid carefully down, his arms supporting her, to the cool, wet metal of the tub. His hot mouth didn't stop. His teeth nibbled gently at her thighs, then closer to her clitoris. She rubbed her cunt against his face until he groaned. She wondered for a moment what he thought of her behavior. He sucked again.

"*Oh, yes.*"

She moaned, unable to think of anything but what Nolan was doing to her as his fingers stretched her so that his tongue could reach more inner spots.

She shivered. She whimpered. She thrashed.

He didn't stop. She could feel his penis, hard against her leg. When he crouched low enough, she could feel his balls brushing against her skin.

She lost count of her climaxes as she gripped his hair to steady herself. Convulsing, she cried from pleasure that was pushing her into near-pain. But his mouth still didn't stop.

His hands knew to tilt her pelvis up to his face so he could move his tongue into her more fully. His fingers knew to enter and stroke her while he lapped at her nipples with his tongue. How could he know that? Did it matter how?

Nell had never made so much noise in her life. She'd never screamed during sex before. But she screamed now. Thankfully the water pounding down muffled her cries or she was sure someone would have called the police otherwise.

"Enough." Panting, she croaked out the words.

She thought he wouldn't stop. "*Oh, God.*" His tongue lashed into her once, twice more, until she shuddered into one last orgasm. By then her head was down, too exhausted to hold itself up. She could feel the tears of repletion and exhaustion trickling down her face.

He stretched his body out against hers and she realized he was still hard. Tremendously hard. She opened her eyes and saw that he was breathing as quickly as she was.

She wasn't sure she could stand his penetration, she felt so sensitive. But she shifted her legs, ready to open herself to him, ready to give him what he wanted.

Then she realized he wasn't trying to enter her. Her hand reached down and touched the tip of his penis. He made a noise, maybe of protest or maybe of desire. He thrust against her hand and she could feel the drops of his sperm there.

But he rested against her, still panting.

"Don't you want to?" she asked. It sure felt like he did.

"That was for you. To be fair." His voice was ragged again.

"Oh." Nell opened her eyes. Her breath steadied a little.

But had she been fair? Wait. If this was still her fantasy, she didn't have to be. She could pleasure herself and have him pleasure her without wondering what he needed.

But he seemed like more than a fantasy. He seemed real.

"Nell?"

"Yes?"

"What is this? A bath I understand."

"It's a shower." Nell thought about having to explain indoor plumbing and decided to do that later. "Now here comes your bath."

She climbed out, her legs still a little shaky, and turned on more water. There wasn't a lot of hot water left, but she didn't need much.

Nolan looked more alert now, healthier. The water must have cooled down his fever a bit.

"Nolan?" She began to scrub his hair, vigorously.

"Yes, Nell?"

"I'm Eleanor Randall. What's your other name?"

"Sean. Sean Nolan."

She liked that name. For a moment she traced the light stubble of dark gold hair on his jaw, the pulse in his neck. Sean Nolan needed a shave. That could come next.

But as he sank against the tub's sides, already half-asleep, she knew she would have to do that for him without his help. She looked at the new scratches she'd made on his body and felt a mixture of shame and intense pride. She'd exhausted him. Involuntarily she looked down.

She'd *almost* exhausted him. His erection still hadn't completely subsided, even though he was now asleep.

She thought she was exhausted herself, but the sight of what he could do made her wonder. "I don't know when this is going to end, but I like this fantasy," she whispered.

In the meantime, fantasy or not, she fervently hoped that he didn't have any bugs on him. She'd come much too close to him if he had.

Though maybe a few bugs would be worth the pleasure.

Nell got out of the tub again and, dripping wet, began to rummage under the kitchen sink. For the first time she felt lucky that she had some flea shampoo left over from the previous tenants. Up until now she'd just wondered if the landlord had ever bothered to fumigate after they'd left.

She scrubbed Sean again. Then she began to scrub herself too. Just in case. And if she touched certain parts of her body more than others while she thought about what she'd been doing with him, well, there was no one else to object to it except the naked, sleeping man in the tub with her.

She wanted to see him in the morning. Their foreplay had been more exciting than anything she'd ever had with any real man, but she wanted it all.

She gave a half-smile. If she knew anything about men, he was going to be desperate for her in the morning.

Unless he was too ill. Or her fantasy ended.

Her smile faded.

Chapter Three

"I don't have any clothes," Sean said once he opened his eyes.

For a moment Nell thought he might object to that. He looked a little stunned. If he did, she was prepared to tell him just how difficult it was to get a groggy man out of a clawfoot bathtub. She hadn't been inclined to search for wearable clothes for him after that.

Then he smiled at her. He had a killer smile. Part mischievous little boy, part pure wickedness.

"I don't mind," he added.

"Me neither," Nell said and smiled back. "But I searched around and found some jogging—I mean, running shorts that might fit you."

He looked at the shorts, seeming a little puzzled. She figured that if she had been baffled by his clothes earlier, then these must be equally strange to him. But he said nothing as he put them on.

What had been baggy on her fit snugly on him. Very snugly. Nell decided she liked that.

She fixed him breakfast, although it was closer to noontime. He wolfed down the scrambled eggs and toast, pausing momentarily to apologize for his lack of manners before wolfing down the remaining slices of toast and cold cereal she had added. To top off the meal, he gulped down a carafe full of coffee. With an appetite like that, he had to be feeling better.

"What is this place?" Sean asked at last, his gaze flicking about intently.

He was feeling more alert, too.

"My home," Nell said, opting for simplicity.

"I've never seen a home like this. I've never seen the things you have in it." He pointed to the computer humming behind her. "What's that?"

"Ummm. Sean, what do you last remember before coming here?" Nell tried to figure out a way to ease him into the realization of where he was.

"I was in Washington. In a hospital. And the last thing I remember is you." He smiled again.

That smile was purely grown-up male wickedness with no little boy charm mixed in. Nell wished she could stop blushing.

"Well, now you're not too far outside Washington, D.C. I live in a town called Manassas. You fought in a battle there."

"Yes'm. I recall that too."

"The thing is, Sean, that—" She hesitated, uncertain how to say what needed to be said. In the end she opted for simplicity again. "Well, you fought in that battle almost a hundred and fifty years ago." Nell looked at the breakfast dishes she was gathering up and not at him. "To be honest, Sean, I don't even think you're real at all. How could you be?"

She didn't hear anything. Not a gasp, or a chuckle, or a shout of dismay. She had to raise her eyes from the dishes to him at last.

He was looking at her, his face a blank mask.

"Nell, maybe you're the one who ain't real," he said at last.

"Of course I'm real!" Nell protested. Then she stopped. Sean must feel the same way she did.

He went on as if he hadn't heard her. "I prayed for you to come and then you came and took me away. But I knew things weren't right back there at the hospital. Everything was like a dream. I think I understand now. I prayed for a chance to be with a woman, just once, before I died. You're my dying wish."

He glanced away, his expression troubled. "Once I do have you, though, you're probably going to go away and I'll be dead."

Nell gave the gasp she'd thought Sean would give when she explained what had happened.

"No! No, you're just my fantasy," she protested. "Once we actually try to have sex together, I'm going to wake up and realize you don't exist. And...and" — her voice softened — "I'm going to be disappointed when you don't."

She couldn't stop looking into his eyes. They were such a bright blue and they held such pain in them.

"Then if we want to stay here, together, we can't consummate what we've started, can we?" he whispered to her. "Otherwise one of us will leave forever."

"Oh."

Nell thought she was going to double over from the sudden pang of combined lust and fear. She sat down. She wanted him desperately. She had the feeling if they stayed together, just the two of them alone as they were, she was soon going to want him beyond desperation.

But she didn't want that at the price of having him go forever. Or, if he was right—surely he couldn't be!—at the price of having herself disappear.

"I don't think I like our choices here." Nell reached out to grasp his hand.

He jerked it back. "No. Don't touch me, Nell."

"Why?"

"I'm not sure I can hold back from you if you touch me. It wouldn't matter so much about me. It might be worth it to be with you, Nell, the way I want to be. But I don't want you to be hurt or—whatever it is that would happen to you."

She swallowed. "Nothing has happened to us yet, Sean."

"That's true."

"If we can't touch each other I think I'll go up in flames, Sean. I've never felt like this before. I've never felt so satisfied or unsatisfied from a man in my life."

"Maybe you better not talk to me either." His voice sounded unsteady.

Nell had a sudden inspiration. "Sean, don't you understand?"

"Guess I don't."

"What we had before—I loved it. I want more, but I loved doing what we did. We didn't get hurt or disappear or anything like that, did we?"

"No."

"Well, if just avoiding actual intercourse will keep us from disaster, there's still more we can do. Other things. Lots of other things." Nell dropped her gaze again and then looked up, almost shyly.

But she wasn't feeling shy. She pressed her legs together, thinking about what they had done and could do. It would be like some of her wildest nights in high school...

Nell remembered that if Sean was real and alive in her time he'd still be in high school.

This fantasy was getting complicated.

Sean was roaming around her living room, touching the computer, staring at the night-light she'd left on in the kitchenette. She watched him walk, admiring his skin and muscles. Kinky or not, she thought everything about him was sexy.

The way his newly cleaned and wavy hair curled against his neck. The deep tan that ran to where his uniform began. With just shorts on she could look at the golden hair on his chest and see how his nipples were hardening...

She smiled. Sean might be curious about her life, but he was also trying not to look at her. His body was betraying his interest.

"Sean, I'll keep us safe," she whispered. "We can still enjoy each other very safely."

He was still so innocent. He didn't understand.

But she could show him.

Nell gave in to her impulse as she watched him debate back and forth within himself. If he wasn't going to touch her, then she'd have to touch herself.

She slipped her short jumper up to her thighs and spread her legs wide. She was wearing lacy underpants today. Somehow she thought Sean would appreciate white lace panties.

She slipped one finger between the sensitive folds and sighed once, loudly, for effect. Sean paused and gripped her computer chair, still not turning around.

That was all right. She knew he could see in the monitor screen. Or at least he could see well enough.

"This feels good, Sean," she told him in a throaty voice that wasn't all for effect. "Almost as good as having your fingers play with me. I love your clever fingers, Sean, did I tell you that?"

She saw how rigidly he held his shoulders, his head still away from her, where she sat with her legs spread apart. Nell couldn't ever remember seducing a young man like this before. But she wanted to seduce Sean. She masturbated almost silently at first, then let out one soft sigh.

"It's lonely here," Nell told him and spread her thighs wider still. "I'd love for you to watch. Please, Sean? I know you want to. *Ahh!*"

She threw her head back and moaned when she saw Sean turn around, breathing hard, his eyes fastened on where she stroked under the panties.

"Help me take my clothes off, Sean. That's all I'm asking. Please help me."

He walked toward her as if he was fighting himself with every step. She licked her lips and he followed her tongue.

"You shouldn't, Nell—"

"No. It's naughty. But you're going to watch me be naughty, aren't you? You'll watch every minute. I won't let you touch. You don't want to touch me, right? So I'll have to do it myself." Nell could barely force the words out.

He couldn't keep from staring. The look on Sean's face combined with her own movements was getting her near climax.

"My panties, Sean. Take them off."

His hands were shaking as he got closer.

"Kneel down, Sean. Take them off while you kneel."

When he knelt, one leg awkwardly balanced, she almost stopped herself. She'd forgotten his wound. Then she saw him reach out and gently begin to take her panties off. He'd forgotten his wound, too.

"Feel how wet my underpants are? They're going to be all stained if you don't slide them off of me," she murmured.

He paused. "Nell, you're killing me," he choked out.

"No. You like it. I can tell you do. I can see how hard you are. But I won't help you take your shorts off, Sean."

His fingers slid under the silky lace and gently tugged. She knew he could feel just how wet she had become. He was breathing hard, almost as hard as she was. Their fingers brushed together because she didn't stop her own play.

When he pulled the panties off entirely, she felt the first clenching of her orgasm come and she let herself go. She thought she heard Sean cry out, too, but she was too far-gone to notice.

When she was finally able to see what was going on, she saw Sean was still kneeling in front of her, his eyes shut and his breath almost sobbing.

"You're going to kill me for sure, Nell," he said hoarsely.

Nell saw that he was hard and ready for her, and suddenly she was sure just what she wanted to do about it.

"Aren't you going to relieve yourself?" she asked softly. "I think I'd like to watch that."

He looked at her, his fingers almost touching the huge bulge in his shorts before snatching them back away. He stood up, looking ready to back away.

"That's not right, Nell. I was taught by my betters that a gentleman mustn't do that."

Nell began to play with herself a little more. She made sure he saw her clitoris being rubbed slowly, rhythmically.

"Oh, but Sean, if we aren't going to let ourselves get closer, you'll need to play with yourself, don't you think? Aren't you desperate with wanting by now?" She kept her voice soft.

He watched what she was doing and she saw sweat forming on his body.

"Isn't it torture not to be touched? If I can't, someone has to, don't you think?"

He groaned. Nell stretched out one bare foot and let her big toe trace its way down his penis through the shorts material. He jerked forward and she pulled her toe away.

"Sean, it's not wrong. Truly, we're going to go crazy if we don't use what we can allow ourselves to do. And I do want to see you spurt out hard for me. Please, Sean. Let me watch... I let you."

Eyes still shut, his teeth clenched, she saw his hand move toward what must be almost agony for him not to touch by now.

"Pull your pants down, Sean."

His other hand swept the shorts down and she saw the head of his cock peek out. He stepped out of the shorts she'd given him and clutched his cock firmly, his hand jerking up and down the length of it fiercely.

"You're so big, Sean," she leaned forward to whisper in his ear. "You're so hard. I just know you're ready to burst—"

"*Oh, Lord.*"

She watched, delighted, as he proved her right. When she was certain he had pumped himself dry, she touched the glistening head of his cock and he proved to her that he still had some more sperm left inside.

Then he sank, hands and face down to the floor, panting.

She laid her hands on his shoulders. "You liked that, didn't you?" she asked quietly. "Admit it, Sean."

"I never did nothing like that in my life. I know the preachers would tell me I ought to go to hell for acting that way." His voice was muffled.

"But if I wanted you to, you'd do it again, wouldn't you?" Nell stroked a tuft of his hair behind his ear.

"Damn it, of course I would, Nell." He looked up, his eyes blazing at her. "Guess I'd go to hell for you in a minute. Guess I will be going to hell for you."

For a minute Nell felt weary from the words he'd spoken. She had only meant to play a little, to show Sean how good things might be.

"Maybe we'll go to heaven instead," she told him, more fervently than she'd intended.

And then she leaned into him and kissed him — a long, deep kiss that, strangely enough, didn't leave her aching for more.

That kiss satisfied all on its own.

Chapter Four

"Nell?"

"What?" She tried not to sound irritable, but realized it wasn't working. She was trying to ignore Sean, which was difficult enough, but she'd also hit a tricky spot in her article.

"Nell, what happened in the war? They can't still be fighting."

"What?" Nell looked up. "Oh. Oh! Sean, I'm sorry. I never thought to tell you." She hesitated, trying to sum up everything. "The Union won," she told him.

He didn't seem to want to know more, which she found odd. Her thoughts strayed as she focused on him. He was sitting next to her coffee table, drawing in an old sketchbook.

"Sean?"

"Yes?"

"Would you mind if I asked you a few questions? After all, you were in the battle I'm researching." Nell knew she was losing her mind. Then again, why couldn't her fantasy man make himself useful in other ways?

"Don't know how much I can help you, Nell. Mostly I was shooting and trying not to get shot." But he put the pencil down. "Things can get really confusing in a battle."

What did she want to ask? Nell was suddenly inspired.

"Here! Come here!" She ran to the cabinet and pulled out the videotape. "Watch this." She popped it into the VCR and turned on the television. Ken Burns' *The Civil War* started.

Sean blinked. "What is this?"

"Television. We use it for entertainment. Now hush and I'll explain later. Watch this and tell me what you think." Nell could suddenly see an entire book forming as she pulled out a sheet of paper. She'd worry about explaining her sources later.

He didn't say anything for a long time. Nell was afraid he was too mesmerized by the novelty of the television to say more. But then finally Sean snorted as an older man began another mini-lecture.

"That ain't the way I heard it." Sean leaned forward. "That old gentleman doesn't know what he's talking about. Meaning no disrespect, of course."

"Why?"

By the end of the program Nell wasn't sure she could write another word. But she felt as if she'd just gotten an entire doctorate course on the Civil War done in one afternoon.

Sean was feeling pensive.

"Never was a Lincoln man myself. I didn't much think about whether the slaves should get free or not before the war. I was too busy trying to scrape a living out for myself, working any odd jobs I could find in the city. All I wanted was to keep out of a factory. I didn't care who the president was," he told Nell. "But I wouldn't wish that on anyone. War is one thing. Murder is another."

"Really?" Nell followed the information she wanted to follow. "Who would you have wanted for president?"

"Little Mac, I suppose. He was good to us."

"How about Grant?"

"I don't know about him. He fought out West, didn't he?"

"I really appreciate you talking to me about all this, Sean." Nell beamed at him.

Sean grunted. He wasn't in the best of moods by now. Watching Nell listen to everything he said, as if fascinated, was making him restless. He'd woken up this morning, alone and aching, on the bed. Though he hadn't wanted to, he'd repeated what he'd done in front of Nell the day before.

More than once.

Maybe she was right and it wasn't a sin. But it wasn't nearly as exciting as when she'd been touching him. And what he'd done wasn't helping to calm him down right now.

He wondered what was the matter with him. He'd gone for weeks at a time in the camp without thinking much about a woman. He'd never felt like this—ready to take someone constantly.

Then again he'd never been with any particular woman before. He'd known sex must feel good but he'd never had any idea that being with a woman could make you feel the way Nell made him feel. He kept looking at her. He couldn't stop.

Right now she'd pushed her short hair up in tufts. He might have longer hair than she did right now, it'd been so long since he'd had it cut. She wore spectacles when she wrote. He didn't know many people who used them and no women who had such things. She wore short, baggy pants that looked a little like men's underpants. She wore tiny shirts that revealed more than they covered. She took her clothes off too, when no decent woman did such things.

Back home, folks would stare at her.

But he wasn't back home and he stared at her because she was beautiful. Even though she wore odd things, she was all female. He'd seen damn near everything about her a man could see and there wasn't a thing he'd change.

Except one.

He'd like to be wearing her himself.

He saw Nell's eyes narrow as she looked back at him and she stopped talking. She licked her lips and he could feel his penis stiffen.

He was caught — a poor fish that had taken the hook and couldn't get away. He didn't even want to. She didn't need to touch him and he was randy. Truth to tell, he'd been ready for her long before she'd noticed he was. All she had to do was be in the room with him.

Or in the house.

Or in the world.

Maybe she didn't even have to be in his world any more. If he was, by some miracle, transplanted back to his own time, he'd never get over Nell. Just her memory would get him wanting her.

She walked toward him, taking her spectacles off. She hooked her fingers, almost lazily, into his shorts. He knew she had to be able to feel what was happening to him, what always happened to him now.

"You have a lot of stamina, Nolan," she told him. "I ought to be too old to keep up with you."

"What do you mean?"

"Please. Don't tell me you can't see how much older I am than you?"

"Never thought about it. You're beautiful. I don't know how old you are." His voice went husky. "I don't care."

"Then I won't tell you." She stood on her toes and brushed his lips, just lightly, with hers. "Shall we try something new?"

"Isn't like I'm tired of the old yet."

She chuckled. "This is a little more risky. But it will be good. I promise. Well worth the risk."

Nell ran her tongue over his lips.

If she was older and from another time, maybe he ought to be grateful. She'd learned a lot. He might keel over trying to learn from what she knew, but he was already grateful for the lessons.

"All right," he agreed. He knew he couldn't help himself.

She pulled his pants down but not off. They tangled in his legs.

"Lie down, Sean. Flat on your back. Remember, I'm in charge. I'm just a little afraid you might not have enough control if you were on top."

"All…right."

He slid down.

"Put your hands under your head. You can't grab. Will you do that?"

For an answer, he put his hands under his head. She straddled him and licked his nipples, very slowly. He hadn't known they could stiffen like a woman's. He hadn't known that they could feel good when teeth nibbled, just slightly, at the tips. He could see her breasts, half-hidden by her low-cut shirt.

He sucked in his breath, felt himself moving his hips upward.

"That's fine, Sean." She nuzzled her face against his neck. "You can do that all you want. Unless I tell you to stop."

Women of her time certainly could give orders. That ability wasn't what folks would call womanly. But she felt damn womanly.

She laughed and took her shirt off, slowly.

She looked womanly.

Nell stood up and he watched her — seductively, with her hips wiggling, pull her shorts down. She took her underpants with her. She stood over him for just a minute, her hands on her hips. Then she straddled him again, closer — very close to where he wanted her to be.

Close but not quite enough.

He could feel the folds of her flesh rubbing slightly against his shaft. He stilled.

Now?

"No, Sean. We're going to get close. Close but — um, no direct hit."

She rubbed herself against him and he thought he was going to have to move, to mount her, to get inside that wet promise she teased him with.

She moved away.

"No. Close, Sean. But only close."

She began to rub herself against him again, little shallow movements against his rigid erection.

This was the worst and best torture she'd managed to think of yet. She danced toward him and, when he thought surely she was going to impale herself on him, she inched away.

He clenched his fists in his hair. If they did go further, she might be hurt if he died. By now that was the only thing he could remember that might stop him from flipping her onto her back and burrowing into her completely.

Her movements were very deliberate. He knew she was moving, using his body against her most sensitive spots. She was using the head of his cock against her flesh and she wasn't the only one who was enjoying what was happening.

He kept feeling the wetness, the warmth of her. He felt her buttocks clenching when he moved his knees upward to support her. He felt her shift her position to something equally maddening but different.

Then he felt her move over him and he could feel the tip of his erection moving up inside her. His eyes widened. This would be what it felt like. Almost.

She allowed him maybe a half-inch and moved out again. Tight and silky and wet and then gone.

"Nell!"

"Sean?"

"Again."

"If you think you can stand it, Sean."

"Oh, yes."

The slow, sensual slide of her body went on. Once or twice, both of them panting heavily, Nell paused and the two of them waited for agonizing minutes before starting again.

Almost heaven but not quite. Not quite enough.

Good. Very good. But not quite good enough.

"Oh, God." At last he could feel the tension inside of him becoming too hot, too overwhelming.

But Nell knew. She moved away, trapping his hips between her thighs as he convulsed under her. That wasn't where he wanted to be but it worked well enough to draw a fierce moan and plenty of seed out of him.

Sean closed his eyes and breathed deeply. That had been good, but now he felt wronged. Only the warmth of her body, tight against his, kept him from feeling completely cheated.

"Nell, I don't know how much longer I can stand this," he whispered to her. "I want you more than I did when I first saw you, and I thought I couldn't want anyone more than I did then."

"This was a bad idea," Nell told him, sounding subdued herself. "We're too close this way. Too close to what we can't do."

He could feel how desolate she was. He felt that way himself. Praying for strength, Sean reached out and held her. She relaxed into his arms, then kissed him, very softly, against his chest.

Sean didn't have the heart to tell her that holding her like this made him long for her even more than he had a few moments before.

Chapter Five

Nothing was quite right anymore. These days Nell threw herself into writing her article since otherwise she and Sean would fight. They fought about everything.

Today she had taken him to the store to purchase him suitable clothing. She'd bought him some underpants, a few T-shirts plus shorts and shoes from K-Mart. Sean had thanked her a little abruptly. As soon as they got back home he looked around.

"Where are my real clothes?" He asked suspiciously. "You've taken them."

"They're in a plastic trash bag. Tightly sealed up. In a few weeks I'll take them out, maybe spray them with something, and the lice will be gone." Nell shut the front door more forcefully than she wanted to. "I don't take things."

If she had thought about the fortune she could get for selling a genuine Civil War uniform, she didn't have to tell Sean.

"Where are they?"

Nell bit back an angry reply and pointed to the kitchen. Sean stalked over to the bag and looked at it.

"I don't know what plastic is," he said, suddenly. "I don't know the names of what I'm wearing now are. I never felt so ignorant in my life."

"Of course you feel confused," she softly replied. Nell suddenly realized what at least part of the problem was and stepped forward to hug him. "Nothing makes sense, does it? And this has been going on for days."

He stepped away from her hug. "Don't touch me. I told you before." His tone was harsh.

That was another part of the problem. Sean didn't want her to touch him — at all — since that last sexual bout.

Nell was starting to wonder if Sean's version of what was happening to them was right. She, after all, certainly seemed to be wrong. This situation was turning into a huge sexual frustration, not a sexual fantasy.

So she returned to her writing instead. Her fingers cramped from the amount of typing she did, but her article was almost finished. Then what? How would they face each other then?

Sean paced. He watched television, but the set didn't seem to hold as much fascination for him as it had at first. She saw that he drew in the sketchbook endlessly the same way she wrote endlessly. They didn't talk, didn't touch, didn't look at each other.

And her frustration mounted until she was ready to scream, to claw at Sean, to end their time together in the way they both wanted and avoided.

Nell stared at the computer monitor and sighed. "I'm going to the university," she announced. "I think it's time I discussed this paper with my advisor. I believe it will be the backbone of my dissertation."

Sean grunted.

"Do you want to come along?" she asked. Maybe they'd feel better if they got out of the house and did something. Anything.

"If you wish."

Sean didn't sound particularly gracious, but Nell wasn't feeling very gracious either. She knew she'd enjoy being at the university much more than being here right now. Without saying anything else, she picked up her purse and the computer printout and opened the door.

Sean followed. She noticed that he took the plastic bag with him. Did he think she was going to spirit that away if he didn't keep an eye on it? But she said nothing as he slung it over his shoulder. He probably needed that connection to his world — the only connection he had left.

Besides, there was no point in saying anything. She was tired of the half-fights and sharp words followed by the retreats into silence. Both of them were behaving very badly.

In the clothes she'd bought him he looked like any other young undergraduate student, she thought. His face was still a little too thin though, and his eyes were a bit too wary for most kids his age. But he looked normal enough. Just as she looked like a normal, somewhat too old graduate student. No outsider could tell what was happening.

Sean said nothing when they came to the grounds of the university. He didn't comment on the length of the drive or the number of students starting to return for the next semester. School was ready to resume. Soon even summer in Virginia would be over.

"I sublet my house for the summer. That means I rented my house for just the summer," Nell explained to him. "Usually I live closer to here. I need to start looking for a place for the fall."

That would mean another tiny efficiency or a room in part of a larger house. Nell was sick of them both. And if Sean was with her, how could she live like that?

What was she thinking of? Would he be with her? And if so, for how long?

"I suppose I could arrange my schedule so I stay there. I could drive in one or two days a week," Nell mused out loud.

That old, ridiculous place in Manassas was the closest thing to home that she had. That Sean had either.

He grunted again.

Nell parked the vehicle and alighted from the car, pulling her papers with her. She knew the article was good. Now she just had to hope that her advisor agreed.

Sean swung into step behind her but when she got to the History Building he stopped. "This ain't no place for me," he told her gruffly. "I'll meet you back here later."

"I don't know how long it will take," Nell gently replied. If Dr. Green liked what she wrote they could talk for hours. Both of them got that way.

"Don't worry," he assured her, "I'll be here."

Nell smiled, a tight little smile. That sounded more like a fantasy man. He would come and go the way she wanted him to. Only she wanted him to stay.

"All right."

* * * * *

Nell left Dr. Green's office maybe an hour or two later, smiling. She'd been right. This was a good article. She could tell from the smile on her advisor's face and the sharp questions she'd been asked that Dr. Green was interested. This day was turning out to be wonderful despite everything.

"Good afternoon, Nell."

"Dr. Astrov! Good afternoon."

Nell had never said much to Darrell Astrov, one of the rising stars in the History Department. His field was modern European history, not a subject she was particularly interested in. But she knew who he was, of course. She was stunned to realize that he knew her as well.

"That must have been quite a chat with Green." The professor swung into step beside her. "I know he thinks very highly of your abilities. Very highly."

"Thanks." Nell flushed a little.

One of Astrov's hands rested on her shoulder, halting her stride. He smiled at her. Then his hand slid slowly, possessively, down her back to the small of it, his fingers almost resting between her buttocks. He circled one finger there, just slightly, and smiled.

"I've heard so much about your abilities that I'd love to see some of your work for myself," he murmured smoothly. "Why don't we discuss it this semester?"

Nell's flush turned darker. There couldn't be any rumors about her and a tenured professor! Whatever gave Astrov the idea that she might be interested in 'discussing' anything with him anyway? She bit her lip.

Maybe even a week ago she might have been intrigued. She'd been available and without a man since her last humiliating mistake with another grad student. A professor's interest would have been tantalizing. Wrong, she conceded, but still tantalizing…

Then she realized why Astrov must have thought she'd be interested. Aaron must have blabbed. She'd thought Aaron was serious about their relationship, or at least enough of a gentleman to keep quiet about what had in effect amounted to no more than a quick lay. Afterwards she had discovered that she was just one in a long series of older women he'd bedded...and not all of those women had been students either.

Dr. Green was Aaron's advisor as well as Nell's and Aaron was jealous of anyone else getting his advisor's attention. Aaron must be not only a liar but a back-stabber too.

Nell's stomach clenched. "Not interested," she said. She tried to come up with a tactful response. "You see, I'm already taken."

"You sounded interested enough in some of the other men around here." Astrov looked affronted. "I've heard you've been 'taken' more than once."

"You heard wrong." Nell's wonderful day at the university was starting to turn into something else. "I don't sleep around and I am faithful. I'm not available."

"You could change your mind..."

"The lady isn't changing her mind." The voice was soft, so soft Nell wasn't sure she'd heard it at first. But despite its softness, both she and Astrov heard the danger in the tones.

"Sean!" Nell turned and twined her arm around him, both out of relief and to keep him from doing whatever he might be tempted to do next.

"I must have been mistaken." Astrov began to retreat.

"Be certain I don't have to remind you how mistaken you were." Sean didn't budge. His eyes didn't leave Astrov's face.

"Young man, I don't respond to threats." Astrov made the mistake of drawing back to stop and salvage his pride.

"I ain't threatening. I'm warning," Sean said, his jaw clenched. He slid Nell's hand down into his and turned his back on the other man.

She could feel the tension in him. Nell hadn't much thought about what Sean had done in his previous world since meeting him. But when he faced down Astrov, she realized he wasn't one of the eighteen-year-old adolescents she knew. He'd killed — others had tried to kill him. That tended to make someone grow old fast.

But he didn't hurt people unnecessarily. She remembered what he'd said: *War is one thing. Murder is another.*

She looked at the set to his jaw as they walked outside and wondered if he was rethinking his position on that.

"Sean, thank you," she ventured.

"For getting rid of vermin for you? That's just something you do without thinking twice about it," he replied with forced casualness.

"Are you angry at me?"

"No. Yes. I'm angry at what's going on here." He increased his stride and Nell inwardly cursed the black dress she'd thought was appropriate to wear when visiting her advisor. It felt too tight when walking so briskly. She couldn't walk faster without ripping the dress. At least her sandals were sturdy enough to keep up with his strides.

They got to the car and Sean rested her back against it, his hands on her shoulders. "Nell, this is eating me up inside. I watched that man put his hands on you as if he had a right to do it—"

"I never encouraged him, Sean. Not ever."

"—and I knew I had more right to do that than he did but I can't. I'm afraid to put even a hand on you anymore or I'll go too far. This is killing me worse than that bullet was."

"Then let's find out what happens next." Nell held his gaze.

His eyes blazed and then he touched her mouth, looking more troubled.

"I don't care about myself anymore. But what about you?"

"I'm an adult, Sean. I'm choosing to do this. Let's both take the chance."

She opened the car door. What she didn't expect was that Sean would slide into the driver's side with her, and as she started the car, he moved to the place behind her, his legs straddling her sides. He flipped her dress up.

"Hurry," he said. "To wherever we're going."

He laughed.

She hadn't heard him laugh like that before. She hadn't heard him happy before.

Sean was used to risks, she realized. Gambling his future was easy.

Next he put his face against her neck and nuzzled, while his fingers roamed into the crotch of her underpants. Nell groaned.

"Sean, I have to get far enough away from here that no one will see us. Safely. You have to stop. I can't—*ohh, God!* Do that again."

The car lurched, swerved, and then held steady for a few miles. Nell realized that this was fated to be the toughest drive of her life. Sean obviously had no intention of stopping anything he was doing.

She laughed herself, and cursed when she almost ran off the road. But although she could feel herself soaking those panties of hers while Sean rubbed her clit in agonizing circles, the frustration was different now. They both were free at this instant, whatever happened next.

Sean was insane with lust. He laughed at her sharp turns and sudden speeding up. Sometimes he let up the pressure of his callused fingertips long enough to pull her hair back from her ears and sing obscene, ridiculous ditties that he must have picked up in the army.

The two of them kept laughing and panting and Nell knew she wasn't the only one who let out the occasional moan.

She finally spied a familiar overgrown driveway. She knew the farmhouse that the road led to had long ago been deserted. Nell's first thought had been to get home as fast as she could, but she also knew another hour's drive would likely get them killed or arrested.

"Here." She managed to say that before Sean reached for her, pulling her bodily over the driver's seat and into the back with him.

"You're so beautiful, Nell." He whispered the words against her throat. "I want you to be mine."

"I am yours. As much as you are mine."

"Then you're entirely mine, Nell. Since I'm entirely yours." Nell tried to remember if anyone had ever said that to her, but then he tore the now thoroughly wet panties from her body and pulled up her dress, sliding it to her armpits.

He just looked, half-smiling still, down at her.

"I like looking at you." He made that announcement as if she didn't know.

"I like looking at you, too, Sean, so take those clothes off."

He grinned, that boyish, wicked grin, and dropped his pants and shirt on top of the trash bag.

Then he was coming down on her, covering her body with his larger one. She heard his breath catch, felt him entering her...slowly, steadily. Despite all the excitement she'd felt up until now, she realized it had been a long time for her. His penis was bigger and thicker than she was used to. For a moment she wondered if he would be able to get inside.

She wiggled a bit to accommodate him.

"Nell, you're so tight," he rasped. "This feels so..." Sean stopped and inched forward again, sweat forming on his brow.

"Good," Nell finished the sentence for him.

And right. Despite the unfamiliar feel, they both knew that the fit of his aroused cock inside of her was absolutely right. He pushed in fully, groaning as he seated himself. When he was in as far as he could go, Nell raised her legs up and wiggled some more until they touched his shoulders. He slid in deeper.

Deeper, harder, as close as he could. His moans reached her ears.

She waited for him to thrust hard, but he did nothing. She could feel him sweating under her fingertips but he didn't move.

"What?" She moaned, trying to move. He was too heavy and she couldn't. "What, Sean? Are you trying to kill me?"

"I just like feeling this," he said shakily. "I like feeling you."

But then some of his control broke and he did move. Slowly, excruciatingly slowly, and then faster and faster yet. Watching him thrust into her was almost enough to give her an orgasm alone. She whimpered.

At the sound his face changed from an almost dreamy wonder of a young man pumping into his first cunt to a fiercer, tauter, almost feral expression. He shifted his weight.

Free to move at last, Nell lifted her hips. Sean answered her invitation. With one hand he pulled her legs up higher, over her own shoulders. With the other he pinned her wrists down. He was bigger than her, stronger, and very aroused.

She knew she was trapped. He wasn't the student this time. He was her master and would do what he wanted. Thankfully she wanted what he desired as much as he did.

He moved roughly, but with careful purpose. Each stroke of his very engorged penis was driving her to desperation. She heard Sean muttering a mix of swearing and endearments. Exciting—so damn intoxicating.

Nell decided she'd had enough teasing. She leaned forward and nipped at his flat nipple. He twitched and the nipple hardened.

Then he gave in.

"*Oh, God.*" At last she felt him slamming hard against her, over and over. All his care was gone by now. Maybe that ought to hurt, he was so far inside her. She felt excitingly stretched instead.

He let her hands go so he could spread her legs further apart. That was fine with her. He entered her again, feeling even bigger than before, banging her ferociously. She scratched and bit and moaned.

And she laughed.

This was how it should be. Nell liked feeling him as much as he did her. She knew she was being consumed by him, just as he was by her.

"I don't want to stop, Nell," she thought she heard him say through the excitement and heat rushing through her. His pounding became relentless, her flesh squeezing and milking his. "I don't want to," he said hoarsely.

But at last he broke. Sean moaned, almost in protest, and then she could feel him spurting and filling her while he was still desperately thrusting, still trying to continue. She squeezed, trying to get everything he had to give. "*Nell.*"

He fell on top of her, exhausted. They lay there— waiting.

Nothing happened.

Nell wasn't sure what to expect as the last, quivering aftershocks of what they'd done ran through her.

She hadn't thought it would be so comforting, the weight of his body lying on top of her and his limp arm draped around her when he finally pulled away.

"Doesn't matter what happens now, Nell." Sean's voice was sleepy and sated and very satisfied. "You're mine. You always will be."

Nell turned her head. She had strength enough for that. Just barely. She kissed his hand, lying on her shoulder.

Then they fell asleep.

Chapter Six

The earth was moving. The thudding dimly reminded Nell of what she and Sean had been doing a few minutes ago. Wasn't it just a few minutes?

She came more fully awake, still smiling, and then realized what was going on. They were asleep on the ground and the earth was moving because of gunfire and distant cannon. Nell turned her head. The car was gone.

She heard men's yells and then shrieks as gunfire rang out.

Sean was next to her, thank God. She could feel him come awake, alert and watchful. His limp arm suddenly tightened protectively.

"I think we're both back," Nell whispered, her eyes wide. "Back to the war."

"Stay down, Nell," Sean whispered back. "I believe we're in for it now."

She watched while he opened the trash bag, which had somehow been sent back with them. He pulled out his clothing. It looked as dirty and bloodstained as ever. Nell swallowed. That was Sean's blood.

"What are we going to do?" She made an effort to sound calm.

"I don't know where we are or where our men are," Sean said. "And I don't have a weapon. So we just have to keep down and keep looking."

Nell shivered as she watched him shove his uniform back on. With each article of clothing he drew on, he became less the man she'd been with in the twenty-first century and more the stranger she'd met at first.

He looked at her as he buttoned up his jacket and said, "Well, at least you're dressed in black. Maybe no one will notice you. You ain't going to look like a soldier, that's certain."

She knew she was the alien this time. She was the one who was lost and out of place. How had Sean kept his senses in her world for so long? She already felt disoriented.

Even worse, she knew what was going to happen next. For once she wished she didn't know so much Civil War history.

"Sean, we must be at Antietam," she said as she grabbed his arm. "That was the bloodiest battle of the war."

"None of them are very quiet or safe, Nell." He sounded maddeningly calm. "But you're going to be safe. Somehow."

Then the earth shaking grew more violent. The cannon's roar wasn't dull anymore.

"Sean!"

He kissed her hand. She watched almost as if everything happening around them was in slow motion. Then suddenly she felt the explosion near them and she was falling, Sean throwing himself on top of her.

"Lord, I don't want her back here!" he fiercely vowed. "If you take her away now, I swear I won't ever ask for her here again!" She heard his voice, barely, after the crash.

"No!" Nell screamed.

Another crash boomed out, closer yet to them both, and everything went black.

* * * * *

Nell woke up, sheets twisted around her on the bed. She fought her way free, half-awake. Sweating, she jolted up straight.

"Sean?"

There was no answer. She kicked the covers away and leaped out of the bed.

"Sean!"

This was the dream, not before. This was the dream, please let this be the goddamned dream, please—

Sean wasn't there. Nell felt tears burning in her eyes that she didn't cry. Methodically she began to look through the house for signs of him.

The uniform was gone. The clothes she had bought for him were gone. He hadn't had much to start with and there was nothing now.

She ran to the kitchen sink and looked underneath. The flea shampoo that had been left there for months was gone from having been used up.

Sean really had been here. She covered her mouth and began to cry noiselessly.

He'd been here and now he was gone.

* * * * *

He'd promised not to ask to see her again. She hadn't seen him. She kept inwardly begging someone, anyone, to let her see him.

Life had gone on without him. School had begun. Her advisor had spread the word that her article and dissertation were good, really good. She could tell that by the way the other professors treated her.

Nell didn't care. She didn't want to write. She didn't want to go to class. She certainly didn't want to teach American history to college freshmen. But that was what she had to do. That was all she had left.

She didn't dream anymore, or if she did, she didn't remember what the dreams were. It was hard to dream anyway since every time she fell asleep she stayed under for only a few minutes at a time.

She found the sketches Sean had made. Beautiful sketches, erotic sketches of her undressed. When she'd seen them she had thought of Sean and desperately masturbated, trying to relive what they'd done together.

That didn't work either. He still didn't come back. As if masturbating would have made him come back.

One morning before class she stared at herself in the mirror. She'd lost ten pounds already. Her eyes had huge circles under them.

"I can't stand this," Nell whispered.

Her head bent forward and rested against the mirror. If she died, maybe she'd see Sean. She'd thought about him fighting, dying this time. She could check historical records to see…

No. She didn't want to know. She didn't want to think of him dead at eighteen, alone and without her. He'd been left at the battlefield without a weapon. He probably had been killed…

No!

But she didn't want to think of him alive either, of him having lived out a full life where he married after the war, had children, grew to a ripe old age. Without her...

"I want to die," she whispered.

"No you don't." The voice was familiar and not quite amused. "You want me."

Nell's breath caught. She was dreaming now. He wasn't here, he couldn't be. She kept her eyes shut deliberately. She knew there would be no reflection in the mirror next to her.

"And you'll have me." Sean's voice held a promise she knew couldn't be kept. But still she felt his hands slide up her legs, under the cotton nightgown she hadn't had the energy to change from.

She felt his face on her shoulder blades. He hadn't shaved and she welcomed the rasp of the stubble.

"Yes, please." Nell finally gave in and pleaded.

If she had finally lost her mind completely, that might not be so bad. Not while she could feel his hands on her body.

He pushed her back onto the bureau, her head forward, her rear up, and she felt him slip into her from behind. She let out one short, harsh sob. It felt so real, it felt like his cock, it felt overwhelmingly good.

He paused, not quite entering her.

"Please," she said. "Do I have to beg harder? You know I will. I'll do anything. Anything you want me to. Oh, please, Sean."

She would. She'd do whatever she had to. If she was going to have one last fantasy, she wanted one where they again consummated everything that they'd started.

"I do love the word please, Nell."

She spread her legs a little wider, wiggled her rear against him invitingly. And then he entered her. She could feel him, eager and hard inside her.

"I'll please you too, Nell." His voice was rougher, almost breathless.

She could feel how deeply he entered her, without preliminaries, without foreplay. That didn't matter. She didn't want any.

Her nipples hardened against his knowing fingers and her vagina tightened against the hard thrusts he gave her. "Please," she moaned the word again. "Don't disappear yet. Please."

"I'm here, Nell."

She wanted this fantasy to last but she was finally, after empty days of being without Sean, too close to the edge. She slid into a shuddering orgasm too quickly. Nell didn't want any of it to stop. Ever.

But even when her first orgasm ended, she could feel him still hard inside her, one finger stroking her clitoris, the fingers of his other hand playing with one of her nipples. She started to peak again.

"Moan for me, Nell. I love to hear that." He whispered it, his breath raspy and tickling against her ear.

She tried not to, tried to hold on. Maybe if she didn't he would stay longer. His hand reached down to play with the outside of her pussy, not quite venturing inside. The other hand pulled and teased at her nipple until it grew harder yet.

She moved her hips forward, jerkily, trying to get more.

He chuckled, a little breathlessly, and fingered her clitoris again before sliding that hand back up under her breast. He had to feel her heart hammering where his hand rested.

"Moan, Nell."

She bit her lip and refused. Slowly his hard cock began to slide out.

No! He wouldn't do that to either of them, would he?

She clenched and shook with the effort of holding him in, but he relentlessly slid still further out. He'd leave if she didn't do what she needed to do anyhow. So she did.

At the first gasp of sound, his cock was shoved back inside, thrusting into her harder than she'd ever felt a cock pound into her in her life. Everything inside her clenched, then spasmed into a fierce, pleasurable excitement. "*Sean.*" She moaned again and felt herself sobbing.

Maybe this wouldn't end. She could hear the sounds they made when their bodies slapped together. The bureau rocked forward, dangerously. Sean went on and on. She was so close to release, so close...

Maybe she would be caught in this fantasy forever.

Then she howled. The next climax was almost too intense. Even then she fought to keep Sean inside of her.

But this time when she finished, leaning weakly against the bureau, he did, too.

"*Nell.*" The sound was gritted out, as though his teeth had been clenched, as though he had tried to hold back but couldn't any more than she had been able to.

He slid out of her.

"Please," she whispered again.

But she knew he was gone.

Nell slid down to the floor and put her head on the boards for a moment, gathering strength. Then she carefully stood up, straightened her clothing, and in that moment she made a decision.

She was going to have to leave this house. The memories really were going to drive her crazy.

* * * * *

She saw Astrov in the hall on her way to her American history class. She didn't flinch, didn't blush. She didn't feel anything because she didn't care. Astrov was the one who avoided looking at her.

Nell took a deep breath before she entered the lecture hall. Having your fantasy man come back for a moment wasn't the best preparation for teaching. She was completely distracted and didn't care what she said to her students. But maybe it didn't matter anyhow. She hadn't managed to summon up any enthusiasm for teaching for the past few days.

She walked briskly into the room. "Good afternoon," Nell told the group. "Today we're going to discuss some of the reasons the United States had a Civil War. Any ideas?"

"Slavery!" One of the earnest-looking women in the front row burst out.

Nell wrote it up on the blackboard. "Any others?"

"The South had the notion it was more important than the United States as a whole and was real unhappy the rest of the nation didn't agree."

Nell's fingers froze on the chalk for a moment. Then she wrote "State vs. Nation." She stared up at the words for a moment more before she turned.

He was there. He looked like everyone else in the classroom but he wasn't like everyone else. He was Sean.

"Any other ideas?" she managed somehow. She wrote whatever the other students said. She didn't know what the words were, couldn't see them.

When she pivoted back to face the group she kept her face turned away from the spot where she'd imagined Sean had been sitting. She might run away from this class once her hour was over, but until then she was going to pretend she wasn't going out of her mind.

Fortunately she had this particular classroom lecture all but memorized so she went through the monotonous motions of delivering it. Inside she could feel herself moistening, feel her nipples hardening. Her stupid body really believed he was there.

Forget about leaving her rental house. Before the year was over she knew she would leave the university, her dissertation, her whole current life. Nell had to get away from everything that reminded her so strongly of Sean. Meanwhile these optical illusions might destroy her, but she didn't want to break down in public.

"Thank you, everyone. Have a good afternoon," Nell finally concluded.

She stared down at the lectern, listening to people gather books and rush on out to the hall. Finally there was no more noise. She was alone again.

"Nell."

Oh, Lord. She'd give anything, do anything, if that really was his voice.

If that really was his hand, holding hers, if that was his body slipping against her, if those were his arms, holding her against him…

"Sean?"

"Goose. Who did you think ravished you this morning?"

"A dream," she whispered. "You left me forever."

"I had you leave the war forever. I didn't say anything about not asking to follow you." He lifted her palm up to his mouth, but instead of kissing it, he licked it. Then he bit down playfully. "I figured you didn't believe I was real from the way you were behaving this morning, so I thought I'd surprise you here. Then you'd know it was true."

"Sean."

She could see him, feel him, hear him, smell him.

"You have an office of your own?" he murmured.

"I share. But the person I share with isn't in today." Her heart was beginning to thud.

"It has a door and a lock?"

"Yes."

"Come on then, Nell."

"Sean." Nell began to follow his tugging hand down the hall, walking faster and then faster yet.

"Mmmm. You want to talk about what I plan to do with you first, lady?"

Nell began to smile. "Are you actually studying the causes of the Civil War with me, Sean? You've enrolled for the class?"

"I don't mind being your student, Nell. Never have." He gave her a sly smile. "You always manage to teach me plenty."

"Sean."

"Yes?"

"There are strict rules about such things." Nell reached the door of the office with him a half-inch behind her. She shut them both inside and locked the door.

"What things?" Sean was already unzipping her pants. They began to fall down—they hadn't been fitting well on her lately anyhow. She'd lost too much weight since leaving him on the battlefield.

"Sleeping with one of your students. I'm not allowed to," Nell told him breathlessly.

Sean cursed a little when the buttons of her shirt wouldn't come undone. Ruthlessly, he pulled one off and played with the lace at the edge of her bra.

"That so?" He looked at her. "Well, we've been there before, Nell." He bit her nipple through the bra cup and she arched up into his mouth.

"What?" she asked, losing track of the conversation completely.

"Doing what we ain't allowed. But I don't think it'll stay that way this time," he said, half chuckling, half groaning as her hands moved against the front of his pants. "I don't need to stay in your class so long as I'm in your bed."

Nell smiled. Maybe it wasn't her best smile but she could feel it getting wider. He was definitely here. Perhaps she could believe this was happening, that he'd stay. "I'm going to fuck your brains out," she promised him.

"Never had any brains to start with, Nell. You'll have to work at this fucking a mighty long time to get a brain from me."

"That's all right too."

Suddenly he pinned her against the desk and pushed just one clever finger into her. She let out a small cry as he probed.

"Sean, I have to be quiet. People are nearby." Nell wondered if she sounded as breathless as she felt.

They could both hear the feet walking outside, the voices raised.

"Nell, you ain't going to care when you scream before I'm done." Sean moved his hands down to hold her more tightly against his cock.

"I probably won't." Nell knew she was a goner when she began to rub herself against him, desperate for more.

"But nothing more happens until I tell you one thing." He bent his head to her ear. "You're never leaving me again. Not now, not in the past, not in the future. I love you."

He thrust into her—hard, possessively.

"I love you too," she moaned.

And she knew that he was right all around. She wasn't leaving him. Ever. He wasn't leaving her. Ever.

And Sean had been right about something else too...

She didn't care when she screamed.

Tears of Amun

Jordan Summers

Acknowledgments

Many thanks to Mom for her futuristic loan. Dad, my family, A, and friends for listening to me ramble about writing. And thanks to my critique partner, Chey. I'd also like to thank Grandma and Edna who always believed in me. I wish you guys were here to see this moment. And last, but not least, to D.M. for being the best creative writing teacher a high school student could ever ask for.

To Si:
The love of my life.

Chapter One
Egypt, 1925

"Hurry up, Charlotte. Don't dawdle." Frustration pinched Victoria Witherspoon's voice until it squeaked.

"Coming, Mother," Charlotte Witherspoon called out, hastening her step, hoping to avoid her mother's ire.

Charlotte closed her eyes and gritted her teeth as she pushed down her vexation. This same haunting scenario had been happening every day for as long as she could remember with little variation. Victoria nitpicked her, continuously chipping away at her self-esteem until it lay like rubble upon the ground. Unable to deal with the pain, Charlotte squelched the hurt that twisted her insides. There was no sense dwelling on it.

Balancing her bag in one hand, Charlotte picked up her skirt to step over the fallen rubble that once was the great temple of Karnak. She'd made it a few yards further when her ankle wedged between two rocks and she tripped, the sack flying out of her hands as she tumbled forward. It was at that precise moment that her mother chose to glance back. Charlotte felt heat rise to her face.

"For pity's sake, Charlotte, do pick up your feet like a graceful young lady should." Her mother's hands went to her hips and she shook her head in disapproval. "How many times must I tell you?"

"Sorry, Mother." She pushed herself up off the ground, ignoring the diggers' curious stares. *It's not like I did it on purpose*, Charlotte wanted to say, but didn't dare speak her mind. It would only make matters worse with her mother, the perfect Victoria Witherspoon, who never did anything untoward. Her mother's manners were impeccable, her taste enviable, and she expected nothing less from her only daughter; which made it unfortunate since Charlotte took after her father Henry, a self-professed, slightly clumsy bookworm. Despite being eighteen, a fact her mother refused to acknowledge, Victoria had a way of making Charlotte feel like an inadequate, somewhat dim child.

She brushed her hands on her skirt and picked up the sack she'd dropped. Charlotte opened the bag, taking a quick inventory of the contents. The book she'd borrowed from the lending library in London was still there, along with her brushes. She held her breath as she examined the brushes, looking for any sign of cracks or breaks. She let out a sigh of relief. Thank goodness the brushes were intact. Charlotte didn't want to receive another lecture on carelessness. Assured she hadn't lost anything she closed the sack and continued on.

Her parents had already slipped into one of the chambers leaving Charlotte standing at the entrance breathing stale air. Their minds were one-track when they were on-site. They probably hadn't even noticed she was missing, not that the oversight was something new. Charlotte was quite used to being considered a nuisance. Instead of allowing her to stay home, curled up with a good book, her mother insisted she be at the dig.

Instead of following, she stepped back into the sunlight, blinking against the glare. Her parents would be in there for the rest of the day and probably into the night, making traces. Charlotte expelled a heavy breath, knowing she should follow them but unable to bring herself to do so. She was itching to get at the book in her sack.

She spun on her heel and made her way around the ruins to a spot near some newly uncovered stairs. Huge sand piles hugged the sides of the staircase, like a giant hourglass that had been tipped on end, lending itself as the perfect hideaway. Charlotte sat on the highest step, drawing out the book. She cracked open the cover, a musty smell indicative of an old tome wafting from the pages. Charlotte leaned forward and inhaled deeply, closing her eyes for a second in delight. There were few things on Earth that struck her as close to the soul as a good book.

Methodically she thumbed through the satiny sheets until she'd found her favorite spot. Pictures of the pharaohs gliding across the cool waters of the Nile came to life before her eyes, their bronze skin glowing against the white linen of their embroidered kilts. Charlotte's gaze caressed the figures, focusing on one man in particular. His chest was bare and unusually broad for an Egyptian. His arms appeared strong, bulging with muscles. The man's kohl-lined black eyes seemed to penetrate the very pages, demanding her attention, drawing her nearer.

Charlotte ran her fingers over the image. Goosebumps immediately rose on her arms. She knew she was being silly but for some reason couldn't bring herself to stop returning to him over and over. She'd loved this man since she was fifteen years old, if it were even possible to fall in love with an image.

She'd even gone so far as to imagine their life together, what it would feel like if he held her in his arms, pressed his lips to hers. Would his lips be firm or soft? Wet or dry? Charlotte knew if she'd mentioned her infatuation with the picture, her mother would remind her that she needed to get her head out of the clouds and meet a nice young man to settle down with.

That would take all your fanciful notions away tout suite. Really Charlotte, sometimes I wonder where your head is...

Her mother didn't need to be standing in front of her for Charlotte to be able to hear her admonishing voice clearly in her mind. Charlotte harrumphed. She knew there wasn't much chance of meeting someone suitable on a dig site in Thebes. All the eligible men she'd considered taking a shine to had been far too wrapped up in trying to make the next big discovery to even notice she was there. Not that Charlotte cared. She wasn't interested in anyone but the commanding man in the picture.

"If only you were real," she muttered under her breath, running her fingers over his still form.

She glanced down at the byline under the papyrus. The Egyptologist who'd written the book had believed the figure in the depiction was King Amasis, but had put a side note at the bottom explaining his lack of evidence and all around uncertainty.

"Little help you are," she spoke to the picture, laughing.

Ever since Charlotte had learned his name, she'd had a vague sense of dèjá vu, but couldn't understand why. Once again she could almost hear her mother *tsking* in disapproval. Charlotte closed the book and put it aside, picking up her brush in its stead. It was time to get to work. At least if her mother wandered by she'd appear to be busy. The air settled around her, hot and oppressive, as she dusted away debris from the half-exposed step with a swish from the brush in her hand.

It had been three years since Mr. Carter and Lord Carnarvon had uncovered the find of the century, Tutankhamen's tomb. She'd been relegated to this small area of Karnak along with her parents, lesser known explorers who strived for one thing only: the preservation of Egyptian history. While the *true* Egyptologists were free to delve into the Valley of the Kings.

She stopped, laying the brush down at her side. It wasn't fair. Her parents had been here just as long as Howard Carter, if not longer. They should have been the ones to stumble upon such a great find as Tutankhamen.

Charlotte sighed and went back to work, toiling deeper into the sand, pushing thoughts of treasure from her mind. She had made three more swipes when her hand struck something hard beneath the sand. Her breath seized and her heart thudded wildly in her chest. Her vision narrowed to where her hand lay still against the hidden item. With trembling fingers, Charlotte carefully cleared the area. The sounds around her muted as she uncovered a small wooden case.

At first glance, it didn't look like much. Perhaps a toy left behind by a child, or a worker's tool kit, long buried in the unforgiving sand. Upon closer inspection, Charlotte changed her mind. She leaned back and glanced around the pile of sand to make sure none of the nearby diggers had observed her making the discovery. All eyes were upon the tasks at hand as they rhythmically worked with picks and shovels.

Charlotte stood, wiping the dust from her hands. She slid the item, along with her brush and book into her sack and made her way to the sacred lake of Karnak. In the late morning the area tended to be deserted. She'd be able to examine her find before taking it to her parents. Perhaps it would be good enough to garner them the recognition they deserved and get them moved to a more prestigious area to dig. Surely if Charlotte accomplished that, her mother would finally see her worth and begin to love her. She sighed. But first she needed to confirm its authenticity or her mother would never let her live it down.

Walking over the fallen stones, Charlotte rounded the columns along the path, her heels clattering over the rocks. She stared at the ruins for a moment, wishing it were possible to see the temple at Karnak in its full glory. The sun, golden in the sky, shined brightly on the water ahead, twinkling and radiant. It was the perfect spot to uncover her treasure. Charlotte glanced at the glass-like surface, shielding her eyes, so that she wouldn't misstep. The area was empty, except for an occasional goose or two that called the Nile valley home. She found a cleared spot near the water's edge and sat.

Sweat trickled down her neck and under her white blouse. Her eyes once again sought the promise of cooling water. The still liquid, tempting in its calmness, called out to her. Charlotte stamped her foot. She couldn't go swimming in the sacred lake. It was forbidden. Besides, it was probably full of crocodiles.

She removed a handkerchief from her sleeve and dabbed at her forehead. The white linen came away with a smudge of dirt across it. Charlotte humphed. Nothing stayed clean in the middle of the desert. She tucked the now soiled linen back up her sleeve and removed the wooden box and her brush from the sack.

The box was no larger than a thin loaf of bread. She gently blew away the sand covering it. The cartouches were well worn, but still clearly visible in their gold inlay. Charlotte stared in wonder, turning the box this way and that, studying the craftsmanship. The wood felt rough against her fingertips from the harsh treatment of the sand.

She looked for an opening. There didn't appear to be one. It certainly hadn't belonged to a commoner. Had a thief dropped it while trying to make his escape? It wouldn't be the first time artifacts had been found discarded in the sand like rubbish. She shook her head in disgust.

She picked up her brush and proceeded to clear away the last remnants of sand until she was able to read the inscription. Charlotte's eye's widened as the words on the box came to life in her mind.

Through the sands of time

By the pharaoh's breath

When the waters rise to highest depth

Then the veils will thin

For two worlds to see

A fated love that must once again be

He who gazes upon the one wearing the Tears of Amun

Shall go on to rule the kingdoms of Egypt

Charlotte almost dropped the box as she read the last words. It didn't sound like a curse, but it definitely sounded ominous. She set the box down, taking a moment to catch her breath. Who had owned this and what were the Tears of Amun? She'd never heard of them, even though her parents had taken care to teach her about all of the legends and pharaohs that existed in ancient times.

They'd pounded everything Egyptian into her head, until she could read and write Hieratic, Demotic, and Hieroglyphs. Charlotte could also speak Arabic, Coptic, and even a little Ancient Egyptian, although she was unsure whether her pronunciations on the latter two were correct, since they had been virtually extinct for over a thousand years. She picked the box up again to examine it further, the words inscribed on top floating through her mind like an apparition. Its presence, a ghostly voice from the past, spoke to her.

Her mother and father had warned her about curses, although they didn't believe in them personally. Charlotte wasn't so sure. Howard Carter had lost several men who'd been there to open Tutankhamen's tomb. Whispers of a curse had spread like wildfire throughout the campsites. Charlotte shivered at the thought.

She heard a splash as something hit the water. Charlotte jumped, her hand automatically flying to her heart, before spotting the culprit. A duck paddled around the center of the lake, unconcerned with her presence, quacking away. She laughed, the nervous sound strained to her own ears. Why was she so jumpy? It wasn't like she'd done anything wrong.

Sweat was now pouring off her. She told herself she'd just go to the water's edge to wet her handkerchief, then come right back. Charlotte went to stand the box on end, when a latch she hadn't noticed before slid free. A golden necklace dropped out on the ground with a clunk. Her breath caught. The sun sparkled off the precious metal, glimmering red on the stones inlayed in the gold. They were teardrop shaped and as crimson as blood. Charlotte gasped — rubies. She ran her fingers over the gems.

The Tears of Amun…

Charlotte heard footsteps and immediately grabbed the necklace, slipping it over her head before someone could spot her. Hanif, one of the workers, stepped from behind a column, his slight body drenched in sweat. She waved to him. Hanif smiled back, white teeth flashing against bronze skin. The man turned silently, as if realizing he'd intruded on her space. Once again she was left alone with her thoughts and her precious treasure.

Charlotte's head was spinning. The gold and jewels around her neck were heavy, weighted. The gold heated her skin, eclipsing the warmth of the day. Lightheaded, she made her way to the water, pulling a square of soft linen from her sleeve. She knelt down near the edge to dip her handkerchief in the liquid. Unable to reach, Charlotte inched closer. The rock near the shore crumbled, toppling her headfirst into Karnak's sacred lake. The air was knocked from Charlotte's lungs as she hit the water.

The lake was hot, stagnant from lack of current. As she struggled to break the surface, Charlotte felt as if a thousand hands were tugging her from below, preventing her from gasping much needed air. She opened her eyes. Her movements slowed as she watched the light from the sun fade and reappear over and over again. Surely her mind was playing tricks on her due to lack of oxygen. She blinked.

Fear surged through her, giving her an added boost of adrenaline. Charlotte broke the surface, sputtering and coughing, trying to rid her lungs of Nile water. Reaching out with both hands she grasped the rough stones near the water's edge. Her hat was gone, leaving her curly brown hair plastered to her back. Her clothes hugged her like a second skin. She brushed a hand over her face, ridding her eyes of water. Geese honked overhead as they flew by.

Charlotte blinked again as she pulled herself out of the lake enough to sit on the stone edge. She scanned the area, a frown upon her face. Once again she wiped at her eyes while her mind struggled to decipher what she was seeing. The columns in Karnak were aligned with intricate carvings at the base, not crumbling and worn. She stood to get a better view. The stones that she'd carefully maneuvered around to get to the sacred lake were smoothed into level walkways. A wall rose up in the distance marking the entrance into the temple area. Charlotte reached over and pinched her hand.

"Ouch!"

Her flesh turned an angry pink upon contact. Well at least she knew she wasn't dreaming. Was it possible that she'd drowned? She glanced out at the lake and saw craft upon the Nile in the distance. They didn't look like the normal boats used by modern Egyptians. They appeared to be longer, thinner. Dark-haired people dressed in white linen stood at the ends of the vessels steering them through the black water.

"Oh my... This can't be... It isn't possible," Charlotte muttered to herself. "I must have hit my head on the bottom." She closed her eyes, resting her head in her hands. Perhaps if she sat here long enough the world would return to normal. "It's only a dream, a bad, bad dream." A cough coming from behind one of the nearby columns jolted Charlotte back to reality.

"Hanif, is that you?" she called out.

There was no answer.

"Hanif, I've had a terribly bad day. Please show yourself." Her voice quivered.

A brown hand appeared to the side of the column. Charlotte released the breath she hadn't known she'd been holding and waited for Hanif to appear. Instead, the most striking man Charlotte had ever seen stepped from behind the column. He wore a white linen kilt with embroidery at the top around his slim hips. The material hung down to his knees, leaving his well-developed calves exposed. His dark eyes, slightly slanted, were lined with kohl, like the ancient Egyptians had been depicted in carvings for thousands of years.

Charlotte frowned. He looked familiar.

His chest was wide and heavily muscled. Gold bracelets with blue scarabs crowning the tops bound his wrists. A gold necklace bearing the shape of three flies circled his throat. Hair of the blackest night hung to his shoulders and had been ornately braided. Charlotte instantly recognized the necklace as a sign of bravery. Why was he wearing it? And who was he?

His face was a work of art, sculpted with high cheekbones and full lips, squaring into a firm chin. His black eyes were heated, intense. His gaze was locked on the front of her shirt. Charlotte watched the rise and fall of his chest, the rhythm mesmerizing, as his fire took hold of her. She glanced down to see what was holding him so captivated.

The white of her shirt had turned transparent from the water. The Tears of Amun were clearly visible through the garment, along with her rosy nipples, which had taken that moment to bead under his close scrutiny. Charlotte sucked in a surprised breath and covered her breasts with her hands.

For a moment more, his gaze lingered before returning to her face. When his eyes met hers, he smiled. The simple act melted her insides.

He was the man from her book.

The same man she'd spent countless hours gaping at like a schoolgirl suffering from her first crush—except he was real. It wasn't possible, *was it*? Had she wished so hard, he'd come true?

Charlotte felt heat start at her toes, rise along her legs, over her knees, gravitating to the apex between her ample thighs. If he could do that with just a look, what would it feel like if he touched her? The traitorous thought entered her mind, sending warmth flaring to her face. She knew without the aid of a mirror, she was blushing.

Her dream man stepped forward. Charlotte hadn't noticed the harpoon in his other hand. She glanced over her shoulder at the water. There was nowhere for her to escape. Her eyes once again found his. He paused, frowning as if reading her thoughts. Charlotte forced herself to smile, willing herself to keep calm until she could figure out what was going on.

Of course, why panic over the fact that my fantasy man has come to life from the pages of a book? It happens all the time. Yeah, and Mother thinks I'm the perfect daughter.

The man continued on slowly, making his way toward her until they were standing but a yard apart. The detail of his clothing was unmistakable. Charlotte had never seen anything like it with the exception of Howard Carter's finds and the book she'd borrowed from the library. She glanced to the ground where she'd left her sack before falling into the lake, but it was gone.

Charlotte looked back at the man before her. A shift of the wind brought his spicy scent to her. Shock and awareness slammed into her body. Her knees weakened as she inhaled deeply. Her senses came alive, zeroing in on the man before her. The juncture between her thighs started to throb. Her nipples beaded painfully. It was as if his mere presence jolted her awake from a deep, deep sleep. Charlotte fought the urge to move closer so she could inhale more of his essence. Touch his bronze skin. He was even more handsome than she'd imagined. The picture did not do justice to this striking figure.

What was she saying?

In all likelihood this man simply resembled the man in the picture. He couldn't possibly be him. That man's name was Amasis and he'd lived over two thousand years ago. Charlotte felt the back of her head, her fingers tangling in her wet locks. There had to be an injury somewhere. She gave up after a moment, unable to locate a wound.

If she wasn't hurt, then she needed to figure out where he had gotten all of the items on his body. She needed to authenticate what she was seeing, and then inform her parents of the find. Charlotte was sure her mother would have a thing or two to say about her appearance, but it couldn't be helped. After all, she hadn't planned to take a swim in the sacred lake. It was an accident, like all the other times…

She held out her hand. "My name is Miss Charlotte Witherspoon."

The man looked at her hand and then back to her face. When he made no move, Charlotte clasped his hand. His large palm enveloped hers, sending delicious tingles racing up her arm. His eyes widened but he didn't pull away.

"It's nice to meet you," she prompted, before quickly releasing him.

Still nothing.

She blew out a ragged breath and ran her hand through her hair. Charlotte wasn't sure why the man wasn't speaking. *Fantasies don't talk,* the little voice in her head chided. She dismissed the thought with a wave of her hand. She needed to focus, but it was difficult with the resemblance to the picture being so uncanny. Perhaps he refused to talk because he thought she'd turn him in for theft. Charlotte glanced at his necklace. For something over two thousand years old, it showed remarkably little wear and tear. In fact, it looked almost new, along with the temple's reconstruction, which was impossible.

"What is your name?" she asked in her best Egyptian tongue, the words stumbling from her lips.

His brows furrowed and then rose as he finally comprehended. "My name is Ahmose." He pressed a large hand to his wide chest.

"Ahmose," she repeated, letting the name play across her mouth. Charlotte tried to ignore the way his taut skin was stretched across a canvas of hard muscle. "I like it." She smiled. At least that answered the question at the back of her mind. He wasn't the man in the picture. His name wasn't common in Egypt, but that didn't necessarily mean anything. Familiar, yet not. She brushed it away, deciding to examine it later.

Charlotte placed a hand over her breast, her erect nipple stabbing her palm. Surprised by her body's strange reaction to the man's nearness, she gulped and forged on, praying he hadn't noticed. "I'm Charlotte Witherspoon."

He stared at her for a moment, his gaze caressing the rigid crests, as if they were still visible. Her skin prickled. Then once again he sought her eyes, his lips now pursing to try and mimic what she'd said. *Well so much for him not noticing…* She flushed as she repeated her name.

"Ch-aaarleete," he said, attempting to imitate the sound she'd created.

Charlotte nodded encouragingly. "Charlotte."

"Ch-charlotte," he said again.

"Yes." She smiled.

Charlotte glanced over his shoulder at the temple of Karnak. Why wasn't it in ruin? As the question ran through her mind again, her head began to swim. The temple was complete, not a stone out of place. There were no ruins in sight. She'd really thought her fall in the water had affected her perception, but since Karnak was still whole, Charlotte was beginning to get worried.

Several men rushed toward their location, weapons drawn, dressed exactly like Ahmose.

This wasn't conceivable. There was no way this could be happening. The man standing before her wasn't her dream. She'd already confirmed that. Charlotte shook her head in denial. She was not back in ancient Egypt; it wasn't possible. She couldn't be seeing what she was seeing.

Charlotte's gaze locked onto his and she swayed. The man grabbed her. The warmth from his palms penetrated her skin just as her world faded into darkness.

Chapter Two

Charlotte's lids fluttered as she willed herself to open her eyes. No longer hot, she felt comfortable for the first time in a while. She stretched, trying to recall what she'd been doing earlier. She'd found a necklace while sitting beside the sacred lake at Karnak. She'd also been talking to the most beautiful man she'd ever laid eyes on, and then everything went black.

Charlotte's eyes flew open. Had he struck her? No, she didn't think so; her head bore no pain. She glanced around at her surroundings. She was inside of a chamber of some kind. Torches protruded from the sienna-colored walls, lighting the area. A ceremonial-looking axe hung between two torches, its gold glittering in the firelight. Shifting, Charlotte looked down at her side. She'd been placed upon a bed constructed of mud brick that appeared to be layered in reed mats and then covered with thin linen. The material was soft against her skin. The odor of frankincense wafted in the air, its spicy aroma soothing.

She turned over, allowing the material to slip down her shoulder and over the fine hairs on her arm like a sensuous caress. A slight scrape over her nipples drew her attention down. Her eyes widened. Her clothes were gone. She was lying in the bed naked with the Tears of Amun around her neck. The rouged pink of her nipples poked out over the top of the covers.

Confused, Charlotte pulled the linen close and glanced around the room again, ensuring she was alone. Had the man resembling the picture undressed her? What had it felt like to have his large hands on her body? Were his palms rough or smooth? Had he taken his time lingering over her breasts, perhaps stroking the tuft of hair between her legs? She squeezed her thighs together to halt the ache that had begun. Charlotte tried to muster outrage, but could only manage insatiable curiosity.

She flopped down on her back and stared up at the ceiling while she tried to make sense of the situation. Leaves had been intricately painted on the mud brick ceiling giving her the sensation of being out-of-doors. The walls were smooth and appeared to be thick, lending to the coolness in the room, the firelight giving them a golden glow. The details were familiar to her, but different. The only time she'd seen anything similar was on a dig and no one in those sites had lived in the dwellings for over two thousand years. It just didn't make sense.

Footsteps down the hall were her only warning a moment before Ahmose appeared in the doorway. Charlotte whipped the covers up to her chin, suddenly feeling vulnerable and small in his presence. He looked as handsome as before with his brown sun-kissed complexion and brilliant smile. His skin had been oiled, carrying the aroma of myrrh.

He opened his mouth and began to speak. The slight difference in dialect compared to what she'd studied had her scrambling to keep up. In over a thousand years no one had heard ancient Egyptian spoken aloud. And no matter what her mind was telling her Charlotte knew beyond a doubt that was exactly what he was speaking.

For a few seconds she just stared in wonder, listening to the words roll seductively off his tongue, her fantasy come to life. From her earliest memory, Charlotte had been surrounded by Egypt and the digs. Her parents had brought her on her first excavation when she'd been barely able to toddle. They'd filled her head with tales of the ancient kingdom and of the great rulers and cities that had once existed. It had been Charlotte's fondest wish at the time to be able to see the cities in all their glory, exactly how her parents had described. And from the looks of things, it had come true.

"Be careful what you wish for, Charlotte Witherspoon," she murmured under her breath.

The man arched his brow.

"W-where a-am I?" Charlotte struggled to speak his language, enunciating every word to make sure she was understood. Her lips puckered as she twisted her tongue around the dialect. Having never heard ancient Egyptian spoken it was difficult to say the very least.

He looked around the room. "You are in my home."

"But where exactly is that?" She glanced at the walls, then back to his face, all the while keeping herself covered.

"The great capital city of Egypt — Thebes." Ahmose's hands moved to his hips and his chest seemed to puff out at the proclamation.

Charlotte's brows knitted. Thebes wasn't the capital of Egypt, but she wasn't about to tell Ahmose that, especially with everything else going on. She didn't want to know, but she had to ask.

"Who is the leader of this land?" Charlotte's fingers gripped the material at her throat until her knuckles turned white.

"The great King Kamose, my brother," he replied, as if she were dense.

Charlotte's mind refused to function. The pharaoh Kamose ruled in the Second Intermediate Period followed by Ahmose the first, who heralded in the New Kingdom. Charlotte's eyes locked with his. She couldn't seem to catch her breath.

This was Prince Ahmose, the man who would be King. Or as the Greeks called him, Amasis, the very man from the picture in her book.

Charlotte brought a hand to her head, trying to stop the wave of dizziness threatening to overtake her.

"You wear the Tears of Amun." He pointed to the spot beneath the linen where the jewels poked through.

She glanced down at the necklace beneath the covers.

"Do you know what this means?" he asked, as he crossed his arms over his chest.

Charlotte wasn't absolutely positive, but from the inscription she had a pretty good idea. Perhaps it had been a curse after all, considering she'd been catapulted through time. With speed she hadn't anticipated, Ahmose closed the distance between them, snatching the cover down while she was lost in thought.

"Wait one minute." She tried to grab the cover back, but his grip was too firm.

He slid his hand beneath the necklace. "It means that whoever gazes upon the Tears of Amun shall rule all the kingdoms of Egypt, with the wearer by his side."

Charlotte's eyes practically bugged out of her head. "It didn't say that," she whispered, distracted by the heat of his hands.

"The last part I added myself," he practically purred. "I care not whence you came. Nor that you speak my tongue strangely. Only that you are here now to become my qefent."

Charlotte couldn't seem to focus. She must have misunderstood him. Had he just told her he wanted her cunt? She blinked, retracing his words, before remembering the other meaning of the word. Surely he didn't expect her to...to become his qefent—his wife?

His gaze heated as it latched onto her nipples. Charlotte's body responded, despite her shock and the need to protect her modesty. With his free hand, Ahmose dropped the necklace and reached out slowly, giving her plenty of time to move away, until his fingertips made contact with her jutting flesh.

Charlotte gasped, then sucked in a surprised breath at her body's response to the warmth radiating from his hands. No one had ever touched her so intimately. Growing up on a dig site had kept her fairly isolated. Had it not been for reading Casanova's "The Story of My Life" she would be completely ignorant. As it was, she'd only managed to experience the sensation of kissing a couple of years ago on her sixteenth birthday. Luckily for her, Victoria had been too preoccupied to know of either event.

Ahmose fondled her nipples, drawing her back from her musings. Charlotte knew she should slap his hand away. But her flesh had begun to tingle, feeling as if a fire had been lit beneath its surface. Besides, being in another time period, things like this held no consequence, *did they*?

He circled her nipple with the pad of his thumb, until it was standing at attention, begging for more. Charlotte's breasts ached and began to throb. She burned for him. He pinched her nipple gently and she moaned. Without thought Charlotte leaned into his hand, seeking his scorching touch. His eyes were locked on her face as if gauging her reaction. She flushed from head to toe.

No matter how hard she tried to fight herself, Charlotte couldn't seem to utter the words to make him stop. She'd dreamt of this moment with him for years. Everything felt so new and exciting, yet so right as if they'd done this a thousand times before. Was it wrong to want to experience something so beautiful with the man she'd loved since the age of fifteen? Her mind refused to think so.

Charlotte stared at his mouth, wanting more than anything to feel his lips upon hers. What he was doing with his hands was driving her insane. She couldn't seem to think clearly, focusing solely on his insistent massage. The ache between her legs had grown to an inferno and she had no idea how to assuage it.

He plucked at her nipple and Charlotte's lips parted. Ahmose didn't hesitate. He swooped down and captured her mouth, drawing out a teasing kiss. Charlotte's body fired off every nerve at once. She couldn't breathe. Her heart was pounding in her chest loud enough to make her believe Ahmose could probably hear it. He tasted of spice and honey, blended nicely with all that was male. She found him utterly intoxicating and was drowning in his embrace.

It wasn't enough. Suddenly there were too many covers on her body. She pushed at them, until he let them drop from his hands and onto the floor. Charlotte sat up to meet his lips. The second her naked body made contact with his muscled chest, her world tilted.

She was on fire. Skin on skin, their bodies slid together as if they were meant to be. He deepened the kiss, tentatively dipping his tongue, then plunging in once she didn't recoil. Charlotte's fingers reached out and grasped his forearms to keep herself from being pulled over the edge into the abyss. He increased the pressure on her mouth, dominating. A growl escaped from the back of his throat, as Ahmose's hands slid over her breasts and around her waist until he could cup her bottom. Charlotte gasped against his mouth, her fingers digging into his skin. They merged once more, the kiss turning fierce.

Within seconds she was being gently guided back onto the bed. Once she was lying flat, he broke the kiss and stepped back to remove his embroidered linen kilt. It fell away from his body. Charlotte's eyes locked onto the rising cock nestled within a bed of crisp ebony curls between his legs. It was as thick as her wrist.

Heat had gathered and pooled between her legs along with moisture. Her lungs heaved in air as he slowly approached the bed and lay down beside her. Every rule she'd been taught about the proper etiquette for young ladies flew out the window when Ahmose touched her nipple again.

His mouth came down on her breast and her nipple sprang to life like a long dormant flower. He suckled and licked, teasing the bud into bloom. Charlotte cried out, shifting her hips in invitation. Her senses were in overload and she couldn't seem to take in everything that was happening. She wanted this man more than she'd ever wanted anything, yet she didn't really know him, only knew *of* him. Ahmose finally took a breath, giving Charlotte a moment to gather her addled wits.

"We shouldn't be doing this," she gasped, as he ran a finger along her arm. "We don't really know each other."

"We have a lifetime to get to know each other." His eyes were intent as he focused on her face. "Our destiny was written long ago. It cannot be avoided or ignored." His deep voice was raspy as he spoke.

Charlotte tried to concentrate on his words, so she could come up with a viable argument. This was wrong. They were wrong. She wasn't meant to be here, *was she*? She shouldn't even be contemplating having sex with this man. *It's all you've ever dreamed of,* the random thought entered her mind. Eventually she'd have to return to her own time. Her parents were probably worried sick. *If they even notice you're gone*, the little voice inside her head whispered. *Why not enjoy the time you have here?*

Even as the thoughts swept across her mind, Ahmose's hands were beginning to do strange things to her ability to reason. He stroked lightly over her skin, leaving gooseflesh behind. His breathing had deepened until it matched hers, calming, reassuring. Charlotte's gaze found his black eyes. They were like molten liquid, shimmering, fiery and scalding in intensity. The temperature in the room seemed to rise within seconds. Charlotte felt feverish, needy. Her pussy ached.

Ahmose smiled in understanding then dipped his head down to the other breast that had been neglected earlier. Charlotte's lids dropped, colors exploded behind them. All thoughts of refuting him and returning to her own time left her head. Her body was his for the taking. She let him explore freely.

Ahmose examined all of Charlotte's hidden peaks and valleys. He couldn't seem to get enough of the fair vision that had appeared out of the sacred lake. He knew better than to question the gods on their wisdom. She arrived bearing the Tears of Amun, which was all he needed to know. He would follow his destiny as was foretold in the stars and bring the kingdoms of Egypt together once again.

He caressed her nipples, the rosy skin as soft as the petals on a flower. His fingers trembled as he lingered over the soft curves of her full breasts. Ahmose dipped between the valley, trailing his finger down toward her navel. He circled the sensitive area several times, before following the same route with his mouth. Her breath seized as he placed tiny kisses across her skin. Ahmose sensed her inexperience and slowed his exploration. He wanted to take the time to cherish this gift, pay homage to her beauty. Praise be to the gods.

Charlotte's full hips bucked as he ran his hand along her leg, scraping his nails over her thigh. She peeked out from beneath her lids, following his exploration. Ahmose marveled at the contrast between the white of her skin against the brown of his hands. The oil from his body added to the glide as he made his way over her flesh, intoxicated.

Ahmose slid down until his head was situated above her mons. The sweet aroma of Charlotte's arousal wafted in the air, mingling with the myrrh on his skin and the frankincense. He inhaled deeply, dipping one finger into her wetness. She gasped. Her eyes flew open, locking on his seeking fingers.

"Such beauty," he murmured lowly. "You are fairer than the flowers growing along the Nile." He slipped the finger into his mouth. "And far sweeter."

Charlotte blushed.

Ahmose swiped his finger again, this time connecting with the bundle of nerves hidden beneath her folds.

Charlotte thought she was going to come off the bed, her body was responding in ways she was unfamiliar with. She had the overwhelming urge to hang on to something, just so she wouldn't fly apart into a million pieces. Ahmose dipped his head and laved the same spot he'd just touched.

Charlotte gasped. "What are you doing?"

"Loving you..."

Her world narrowed to his insistent mouth. Nothing else matter or existed. Ahmose shifted again until his body was positioned between her thighs. He dove between her legs, lapping and thrusting at her clitoris with his tongue.

Charlotte could feel tension building inside her, winding tighter and tighter, as if drawing her near a razor's edge. Her hips were moving of their own volition, trying to match his probing. Charlotte grasped his head, her fingers sinking into his ebony hair as her pussy pulsed with need. It seemed to be all the encouragement Ahmose required. He became frenzied, feeding at her woman's center, plunging into her drenched channel.

The blood was pounding so loudly in her ears Charlotte could hardly hear. "Please," she begged, not at all sure exactly what she was asking for. She closed her eyes against the sensation. Her hips thrust against his mouth, wanting, needing, and desiring something more.

Ahmose sucked her clitoris between his teeth and purred, vibrating the sensitive flesh, until a dam seemed to burst inside of her. Charlotte cried out again as she slipped over the precipice and into the unknown below. Her body tingled from head to toe, her legs shaking around his head. Charlotte couldn't seem to stop twitching, as contraction after contraction of pleasure rocked through her.

When Charlotte finally opened her eyes and could focus, she glanced up into the smiling face of Ahmose. His grin said it all. He was more than pleased with what he'd done to her. He positively glowed. The second Charlotte recalled exactly what she'd let him do, her gaze dropped. She didn't think she'd ever be able to look Ahmose in the face again. He'd kissed her and she'd turned positively wanton in his arms, thrusting her sex in his face like a dog in heat. What must he think of her?

As if reading her thoughts, Ahmose shifted up, until his hips were cradled within her own. Charlotte's gaze flew up, meeting his eyes. She could feel the hard evidence of his arousal, digging into her soft belly. He held her captive as if willing her to recognize the woman she was about to become.

"I'm not so sure I can do this," she whispered.

He smiled again, his cock bucking against her skin. "We have been made for this since the beginning of time, my precious jewel. Trust in what is to be."

Ahmose shifted his hips until his cock lay poised at her entrance. It took every fiber of his being to keep from thrusting forward and taking what was rightfully his. He wanted Charlotte to go on this journey with him. He slipped his hand between their bodies and began to rub the crown of his shaft over her slick folds. She sucked in a breath, then bit her lip. Ahmose allowed the head to slide into her entrance — it was like heaven, tight, hot, and oh so pleasurable. Charlotte's eyes widened in surprise, but did not show fear. The fact made him prouder than it should have.

"This will hurt but for a moment, my love," he murmured against her cheek as he placed kisses upon her face.

Ahmose slipped his cock in a few more inches, until he encountered her thin barrier. Her velvet channel was molten as it gripped his length, drawing him deeper inside her sheath. There was no easy way to aid this first joining. Ahmose leaned over, latching onto her nipple with his mouth, and thrust forward at the same time. A pain-filled gasp escaped from Charlotte's lips, but he continued to embrace her, lapping at her nipple soothingly. He held his body completely still, the muscles in his back and buttocks straining against the urge to seek his completion.

Charlotte couldn't breath. The pain...the pain she'd felt moments ago was fading and turning into something else. She felt full, stuffed, and unable to move. Ahmose was in her, surrounding, dominating her with his presence. Before this, she hadn't thought their joining possible, but now her body was adjusting, accepting, and welcoming his cock as if it belonged. He slowly released her nipple. Just when Charlotte thought the sensations would cease, he moved, a gentle thrust at first, testing her. She gasped, but instead of pain she felt only pleasure.

Her nipples beaded against the scrape of his hairless chest as he rose up to support himself with his elbows. The small movement brought him deeper inside of her, nudging her womb. Her channel flooded once again, accommodating his size.

"Are you all right?" he asked, little lines creasing his face while concern marred his brow.

"I'm fine. It feels..."

He thrust again. And passion exploded inside of her.

"Wonderful." The word came out on a sigh.

He smiled down at her as he picked up speed. His cock plunged deeper, his rhythm picking her up and carrying her along on a wave of desire. He rocked sideways, massaging a spot inside of her that was almost as sensitive as the little nub on the outside. Charlotte allowed herself to fall into the feeling. Ahmose's hips bucked and surged, pistoning faster and faster. Charlotte's lids started to fall.

"No," he cried. "I want you to look at me when you come again." The muscles in his neck strained. "I want you to know who will be your king."

Charlotte opened her mouth. She wasn't sure if she was about to protest or concur. Ahmose took that moment to dip his tongue inside, circling and twisting with her own. The now familiar throbbing sensation started low in her belly. Charlotte's grip tightened. Ahmose drove deep again and again, centering his effort at her very core. It was all that was needed to hurl Charlotte into another orgasm. She pulled back and screamed, all of her muscles tensing at once, her pussy milking his cock.

The second her sheath grabbed him it was over for Ahmose, and his seed began to spill from his body. Her unrestrained response sent him into oblivion. His hips continued to move as the last of his essence was emptied into the center that would soon hold new life. This wonderful gift from the gods was his, all his and he had no intention of ever letting her go.

Before he'd given it another thought, Ahmose decided they would wed before the celebration of the Opet. Charlotte would become his princess and then later his queen.

Charlotte was seeing stars across the handsome face above her. He was everything she'd ever imagined in a lover and more. His passion had been limitless. They were still joined, but the fact no longer held embarrassment, only joy. Her heart swelled as she felt him throb inside her.

This man, this prince, had wanted her, Charlotte Witherspoon, the woman who'd fallen in love with a picture, when he could have had anyone in the kingdom. The thought was empowering. She reached up and moved a satiny braid of his hair over his shoulder, so that she could see his face clearly. He was grinning down at her, possession burning in his eyes.

A loving curve touched Charlotte's lips.

"What brings you joy?" His smile reached his eyes.

She ran her finger along his jaw. "I was just thinking how lucky I am to have found someone like you to be my first lover."

His expression darkened, storm clouds filling his eyes.

Charlotte dropped her hand away. "Did I say something wrong?"

"You shall have no other lovers from this day forth. You have given yourself to me. I have planted my seed. It is done." He slipped from inside her and slid off her body.

Suddenly Charlotte felt cold, empty. She frowned as she tried to think about his words. "You can't expect me to stay here. I don't belong in this t—"

"I shall hear no more of this." He fastened his kilt in haste. "You are to become my wife."

"Wife!" Charlotte sat up, scrambling for the covers at the same time. "I can't become your wife. I have to get back."

For a moment an expression of confusion crossed Ahmose's face, then just as quickly it cleared. "I will offer the proper gifts, ones fitting for a soon to be queen. Tell me what land I must send them to and it shall be done."

"Queen? Land?" Charlotte was struggling to keep up—first his wife, then his queen? The pieces of the inscription fell into place like an iron latch. "Ahmose, there's been a terrible mistake. The Tears of Amun aren't mine."

He stared, aghast. "You stole them from their rightful owner?"

Charlotte's mouth dropped open. "I would never."

Relief flooded his features. "Then it is settled. We wed in a few days, just in time to join the Opet festival."

She simply stared, unsure of what to say next.

"I will return with some clothing, since your old garments were…unsuitable." Ahmose slipped from the room before she could respond.

Charlotte watched his retreating back until he disappeared around a corner. She had to explain, try to convince him to call the wedding off. Her heart sank. It would do no good falling in love with the man, when in the end she'd have to leave him.

Who was she trying to kid? She'd fallen for Ahmose years ago when his name had been Amasis and he'd only been a picture on a page. The thought of never seeing him again bothered Charlotte more than she cared to admit. After today, how was she going to live without him? The thought was too painful to contemplate.

Chapter Three

Charlotte lay on the bed, sated, awaiting Ahmose's return. As much as she liked being here with him and experiencing the joys of lovemaking, she had to find a way out of his time and back into her own. If there was a way in, there had to be a way out. Besides, if she ended up staying, history could be irrevocably altered. The question was…how to get back.

She was playing with the gold around her neck when Ahmose returned. He brought her delicate linen, much like what he wore, and carried a wooden chest, laminated in precious gems and mother of pearl, which he proceeded to open. Charlotte almost fell off the bed when she saw the jewels and mass of wealth he displayed. Only in Tutankhamen's tomb did gold like this exist. Her heart thudded as he picked up a ring of gold. Charlotte stared as he slid the ring onto her finger. Tears sprang to her eyes as she realized no matter how much she wanted this, it could never be.

"If you do not like this one, I can get you another." He hesitated, then began to dig through the jewelry.

She swiped at the tears with the back of her hand, then reached to still his movements. "It isn't that. The ring is lovely."

"Then why the tears?" He ran the pad of his thumb over her cheek, wiping away the moisture.

"I'm a little overwhelmed." She shrugged. "I'm a long way from home and not sure how to get back."

He smiled. "Egypt has some of the finest trackers in the land. I'm sure they will find your home, if that is your wish."

Charlotte laughed. She doubted very much if anyone here would be able to find her home. Ahmose reached back in the chest and was once again looking through various items. He picked up two ruby earrings and grinned as he held one up to the side of her face.

"Perfect. They match the Tears of Amun and the fire that lights your eyes."

Charlotte brought his hand to her mouth. She placed a chaste kiss upon his knuckles, before allowing him to hang the earrings from her ears. Ahmose helped her get dressed, showing Charlotte how to tie the linen about her. By the time he'd finished she felt like a true Egyptian princess. He slipped sandals onto her feet and then led her out of the room.

They walked down a narrow corridor into a courtyard. A tree grew in the center, lending shade to the hot afternoon sun. They continued on until reaching the main entry, where several women sat.

"These are my servants. They will assist you with anything that you might need." He swung his arm wide, indicating everyone in the room.

"I'm not sure I need so much help." Charlotte stared at the women, giving them a tentative smile.

Ahmose squeezed her hand. "This is how I live in Thebes. Later we will visit my brother's harem. He will be anxious to meet you."

Charlotte pictured a houseful of naked women running around feeding the men grapes. She knew she was just being childish. This was how ancient Egyptians lived — at least the ones who had money.

"Do you have a harem?" she asked without thinking.

Ahmose turned to her. "You are standing in my harem."

Charlotte's gut clenched. "B-but I thought these women were your servants, not your wives." Her gaze traveled over their faces once again, jealously scrutinizing their appearance.

Ahmose tipped her chin back until she was looking at him. "A harem is private quarters. A retreat. These women are my servants. You will be my wife."

Charlotte leaned into the warmth she saw in his eyes. His gaze held so much promise, so much...*love*? She knew it wasn't possible, but there it was in the depths of his black eyes — love. He'd just met her. There was no way he could be feeling such things. It couldn't happen, she wouldn't allow it.

What are you going to do, rip out his heart? The thought had her cringing. If she stayed here for much longer it could very well happen when she left.

"Come, my love. Let us eat." Ahmose clapped his hands twice and the women scattered in all directions.

Within moments a linen throw had been tossed on the floor and an area had been set up for them to dine. Bowls containing dried fish, fresh fruit, and bread were laid upon the blanketed floor. Cushions stuffed with goose feathers were brought for them to sit upon. A thick beverage was poured into two cups; the servants tossed in dates and stirred in honey. One was handed to Ahmose, the other to

Charlotte. He held up his cup and waited for her to do the same.

"Here's to my future bride." He grinned and took a sip.

Charlotte smiled back and drank from her cup. The brew was thick and grainy as it slid down her throat. She'd read about this drink, but this was the first time she'd ever tasted barley beer. >From the darkness and the taste of the brew, it was quite a potent batch. As Charlotte drank, her muscles begin to relax. Ahmose tore off a bit of the crusty bread and handed it to her, then passed the fish.

"How long have you lived here?" Charlotte asked, sounding too eager. There was so much she wanted to learn, so much she wanted to see.

"Many years." He swallowed the bread he'd been chewing. "My brother and I were raised in the town of Gurob, near the Fayuum oasis on the edge of the desert. My family has another harem palace there. Perhaps you'd like to see it sometime?"

"I'd love to." Charlotte couldn't hide the enthusiasm in her voice.

This whole experience was like a dream come true. She was afraid at any moment she'd awaken and it would all be gone. Charlotte's heart squeezed in her chest and for a moment she had to look away, unable to gaze into Ahmose's eyes. After a few seconds, she composed herself enough to continue their conversation.

"Would it be possible to view the city of Thebes today?" *Did she really have time to sightsee? But how could she be here and not?*

Ahmose was watching her closely, not missing the moment her eyes misted over. "I think that would be possible. My chariot is housed with my horses."

Charlotte's green orbs lit up in excitement.

"Tell me, my love, where do your people hail from?"

Charlotte stilled mid-motion from picking up her cup to take a drink. She'd hoped they could avoid this question. She put the beer down, her teeth worrying her bottom lip. Finally she released a breath.

"I come from lands far to the north, beyond the realms of Egypt, across the seas." She began picking at a loose thread on her kilt.

"How did you come to be here?" Ahmose took a drink of his beer, and then set the cup down.

That was a very good question and for the life of her, Charlotte wished she had the answer. She couldn't exactly blurt out she was from a different time. Ahmose would probably have her stoned to death. So she fibbed. "My people left me on their journey further south."

His brows furrowed and anger flashed in his black gaze. "How could they leave the bearer of the Tears of Amun and one so fine and beautiful as you?"

Charlotte glanced down at her lap, then back up into his face. "Where I'm from the Tears of Amun don't have the same meaning."

"How can that be?" He shook his head. "The gods would not allow it."

"My people have moved away from the gods. They are not as well thought of as they are here."

Ahmose gasped. "This cannot be. It is blasphemous." He rose from the floor, his hands going to his hips. "I do not understand your people."

Charlotte chuckled. "If it makes you feel any better, I don't either."

"Come." He held out his hand. "Let me show you Thebes."

Charlotte let Ahmose pull her to her feet. He led her behind the palace to a stable. There were many horses of various colors in a paddock, and off to the side stood five chariots.

"Are those all yours?" She pointed to the chariots.

Ahmose grinned. "They are mine and my family's. The one on the end is my favorite."

Charlotte could see why it was his favorite. The front of the chariot was inlaid in gilded gold. The wood paneling at the sides had been painted and carved with depictions of Ahmose defeating his enemies in battle. The vehicle was so ornate, Charlotte wondered if they should really be riding in it.

"Come." He tugged her arm, pulling her forward. "What color do you prefer?"

Ahmose nodded toward the horses. Her gaze flew to the massive horseflesh prancing around the ring, kicking up sand. A dappled gray stallion bucked and reared, nickering loudly, drawing her attention from the others. His long white mane and tail glowed in the sunlight. The muscles in his sleek body rippled with unbridled strength. He tossed his head in her direction, then snorted.

"Him." She pointed to the stud.

Ahmose smiled again. "He's my favorite. I call him Hasani. It means handsome."

Charlotte glanced back into the paddock. "It fits him," she said, laughing.

Ahmose whistled, three quick bursts of sound. Hasani's ears twitched then perked up. Ahmose repeated the whistle and the stallion trotted over to stand next to him.

"That's a great trick." She nodded toward the horse. "Do they all do that?"

It was Ahmose's turn to laugh. "Only when they feel like it, I'm afraid. They are much like women—they do nothing unless they want to."

Charlotte opened her mouth to protest.

Ahmose winked, immediately soothing her ruffled feathers.

Heat rose in her cheeks. How did he calm her so easily? She shook her head and rolled her eyes. Ahmose leaned in and kissed her on the cheek, then signaled for his servants to ready the chariot.

Moments later, wind whipped through Charlotte's hair as they raced down the roads of Thebes. Several people lined the streets to see the chariot pass by. Hasani's slashing hooves and the chariot's wheels clattering over the stones sent dust whipping behind them. Ahmose had her pressed to the front of the chariot, his weight balanced behind her as he guided the conveyance. Charlotte could feel his cock against her back, as it grew and lengthened with every move she made.

She felt strong, powerful, like a woman. Not the klutzy girl she'd been when she left her time. She wiggled and his shaft grew, hard and urgent. He groaned, dropping one hand to his side. Suddenly she felt a tug at the back of her kilt and then a breeze. She froze.

"What are you doing?"

He pressed his lips to her ear. "Spread your legs a little more." He rasped his fingernails over her silky skin, leaving gooseflesh in its place.

Without thinking, Charlotte did, exposing her cunny to his machinations. Ahmose slipped inside her from behind, filling her completely, before taking up the reins once more. Each bump they hit drove his thick cock deeper into her core. The slow torturous movements seared her, fanning out across her body like licking flames. Charlotte tried to wiggle around so she could see him.

"Don't move." His hips pressed against her, holding her to the front of the chariot. The pressure caused her clitoris to throb. "Or someone may notice," he whispered, taking care to steer the chariot over the uneven road.

She couldn't breathe or think, only feel as she gripped the chariot, as he continued to slip in and out of her wet pussy. Her nipples stabbed against the linen, rasping. Ahmose placed the reins in one hand and circled her clitoris with the other. His thumb probed and stroked, feathering the nubbin with glorious attention. Charlotte's cunny pulsed once, then she came hard. Her scream was muffled, swallowed by his rapacious kiss. He thrust rapidly, driving into her like a man possessed, before following her shortly thereafter.

This was one chariot ride she wouldn't soon forget. Deliciously sated, it took Charlotte a few moments to realize that they had passed the temple at Karnak. Sand dried out her mouth, but she didn't want the ride to end. She breathed in, the heavy spice from nearby kitchens perfumed the air. Charlotte could almost taste the food from the odor alone.

Ahmose slowed Hasani to a trot, his hooves clopping, as they echoed off the walls of the many shops and homes tucked throughout Thebes. The sun was setting on the horizon, brilliant rays of red, purple, and pink, catching the sails from the boats on the Nile in its fading light. Charlotte sighed and snuggled deeper against Ahmose's chest, a smile planted on her face. She could get used to this way of life quite easily. The thought should scare the wits out of her, but it didn't.

They returned to the palace as the last rays of light dropped below the horizon. Ahmose helped her down from the chariot and handed the reins to one of his servants.

"Come, it is time to break for the night." He guided her along the path, his big hand resting on the small of her back.

Charlotte could feel heat from his touch through her clothes as if he'd placed a hot iron against her skin. Her stomach knotted in anticipation. Ahmose didn't look at her, but she could tell he was aware of her slightest movement. They entered the palace, passing through the main parlor area, out into the courtyard beyond, and then into the chamber that held his sleeping area.

Charlotte couldn't seem to remember how to walk. She tripped over one stone and then another, until Ahmose clasped her elbow, steadying her.

His singeing touch only served to intensify the emotions she was feeling. Her skin burned. Was it possible to spontaneously combust? At the moment, Charlotte thought so. She tugged at the material near her neck. Her clothing felt as if it were smothering her, every fiber woven together to add to her discomfort. She glanced out of the corner of her eye and caught Ahmose smiling at her. She didn't think this situation was in the least bit funny.

"Are you warm, my love?" He leaned in until his lips were almost upon her ear.

Charlotte shivered.

"I can help," he all but growled. "Perhaps you'd like some water?" His eyes twinkled in the torch-lit hallway.

She shot him a look. Ahmose didn't even flinch. He was enjoying the fact that he could toy with her. He knew she was at the mercy of her hormones. Well two could play that game. Charlotte knew she may not have much experience, but if the chariot ride was any indication, she wasn't completely without means.

Charlotte ran her hand along Ahmose's arm, pausing at his rounded shoulder. His muscles tensed beneath her fingertips, but he did not pull away. She continued her innocent exploration onto his chest, his skin searing her hand. When she reached the flat disc of his nipple Charlotte rubbed it between her thumb and forefinger. Ahmose's breath caught and his eyes flashed.

"You are playing a dangerous game, little one. Everyone knows not to tease a lion." His grin was absolutely feral.

She gave him a wide-eyed look as if to say she didn't know what he was talking about, and worked her hand lower. Charlotte's fingers slid over the ridges of Ahmose's muscled stomach. When she arrived at his navel, he flinched. This was fun. Having this big strong male at her mercy was more enjoyable than she'd thought it could be.

She circled his belly button, allowing her nails to lightly scrape his skin. Charlotte slid her hand along his belted waist. She glanced down and saw the evidence of his arousal pushing against the white linen of his kilt.

His cock grew thicker the longer she stared. Finally Charlotte couldn't resist. She slipped her hand over his shaft. Ahmose froze for a second and then pressed his length into her hand. Charlotte's fingers wrapped around his cock. His breath came hissing out.

"Are you trying to cause injury to me?" he asked, his voice hoarse.

"No." Charlotte went to pull her hand back, but he stopped her.

He took a deep breath and let it out. "I was trying to be gentle with you since today was your first time. But such torture is driving all honorable thoughts from my head." His body trembled beneath her touch. Ahmose's gaze bulleted to her lips. "Ra, give me strength." He groaned and leaned down, pressing his lips to hers. The kiss was gentle, not rushed, as if they had all the time in the world.

She didn't think there would ever be a moment when she would tire of his embraces. Her knees quivered as he deepened the kiss, his mouth firming as hers grew more yielding. His tongue swiped at her lower lip, seeking entrance. Charlotte opened for him, welcoming his spicy taste. His hands moved to her shoulders. He rested his palms there for but a moment then pulled her closer without shifting her hand from his shaft.

Charlotte felt his cock pulse against her fingers. Tentatively she stroked down, unsure of exactly what to do. He bucked his hips in encouragement. She reversed direction and slid her hand back up his length. Ahmose growled against her mouth. Feeling confident, Charlotte stroked him again, this time without pausing. His grip on her shoulders increased, but he didn't break the kiss. She increased her speed, enjoying the feel of his fullness in her hand.

Sweat broke out on Ahmose's brow. He was trying very hard not to drag her to the ground right in the hallway. His fingers bit into the material around her shoulders, trying to anchor his need. She slid her silken fingers over his crown and gently applied pressure. He clenched his jaw against his instinctive response to thrust. If she kept this up for much longer he was going to spill his essence. Unable to take a minute more, Ahmose pulled back from the kiss, gasping.

"Woman, you have tortured me long enough."

He grabbed her hand, pulling Charlotte more forcefully than he'd intended toward his bedchamber. He was loosening the ties holding her kilt together before they even reached the door. Her lips were swollen and red from his kisses. Ahmose snatched up a wisp of her curly hair and brought it to his nose. She smelled of wind and sunshine. Her eyes were wide and sparkling in the torchlight.

He released her long enough to shut the door. He then walked to a small bowl containing myrrh and frankincense, crushing the resin in his hand until the room smelled of spice. He turned in time to see Charlotte remove the remaining linen from her body. Ahmose's breath caught. Her skin glowed like alabaster. The rose of her engorged nipples called out to him. The dark thatch of curls between her thighs had already begun to dampen, glistening like a beacon in the torchlight.

She wanted him, just as much as he wanted her.

His mouth watered at the thought of sinking between her spread legs and sampling of her bounty once again. Tasting her juices as they burst from her body in ecstasy. His cock strained beneath the material of his kilt, demanding to be released. The Tears of Amun adorned her neck, while the ruby earrings flashed fire against her ears. Ahmose swallowed hard. He longed for the moment to last for this lifetime and into the next. He fisted his hands at his sides to keep from reaching out and taking her. He wasn't done looking his fill.

Charlotte shifted under his intense gaze. Inside her a fire raged that only he could douse. She had no idea what possessed her, but she brought her finger to her mouth, gave it a quick lick, then ran the same finger around her nipple, leaving a trail of moisture. The areola puckered. Ahmose's nostrils flared and his body trembled. He removed his kilt in a few seconds flat and was upon her. This time his kiss was aggressive, hungry. He pushed past her defenses, attacking her mouth savagely.

Charlotte was lost. His hands seemed to be everywhere at once, groping, pinching, squeezing, and caressing. He kneaded her flesh, stroking her mons at the same time. Charlotte moaned against his mouth. He dipped one finger into her drenched channel and began to thrust in and out. When her hips joined in the rhythm he added another finger. The tension in her abdomen was building, drawing nearer to release. She tightened her inner muscles, holding his hand in place, seeking the relief he promised.

Just when she was about to slip over the edge he broke the kiss and pulled out of her, maneuvering her toward the bed. Charlotte went to lie down, but Ahmose stopped her. Instead he spun her and bent her forward until only her elbows rested on the reed mats. Charlotte's heart leapt to her throat and her breath seized. Visions of the chariot ride passed through her mind, fueling her need.

For a few seconds she stood there, her bottom raised in the air toward Ahmose. Then she felt his cock as it brushed against her cheeks, hard like granite, yet soft as satin. He didn't try to enter her. He just continued to stroke over her skin, teasing the edge of her pussy lips. Charlotte pushed back in encouragement. He laughed and held her hips still. He leaned down and placed a kiss on each globe. Charlotte trembled.

Ahmose stood, and then bent over her. "You have punished me long enough," he whispered against her hair. "Now it is my turn."

Excitement thrummed through her. She could feel her nipples bead to the point of pain. Her cunny was saturated to the point that her dew was about to run down her legs. And not for one second did Charlotte care, her sole focus on the large cock between Ahmose's thighs, and the sexy voice vibrating through her senses. Her clitoris twitched as he slid the crown over her nub, his heavy sac brushing her leg. Charlotte bit her lip to keep from crying out, or worse yet, begging.

Ahmose stuck the tip of his cock in her waiting entrance, his fingers digging into the flesh of her hips in preparation. He would torture her for a few minutes more and then fuck her senseless. He pulled out and she whimpered, opening her legs wider.

"Is there something you wanted to say to me, my love?"

Charlotte groaned. "No."

He dipped inside once more, this time releasing one hip so that he could reach around and massage her clitoris. Charlotte whimpered, her legs almost giving out. Ahmose circled her stomach, holding her up with one hand. He rocked forward again, his shaft sliding past her entrance and along her crack. She bucked within his hold, her cunny demanding his cock.

"Please," she begged.

"That's all I wanted to hear." His voice was gravelly as he released her long enough to grab her hips once more and plunge in from behind, branding her.

Charlotte screamed as an orgasm racked her body, pulsing and throbbing as wave after wave hit her. She could hear the suction noise as Ahmose drove his cock in and out of her pussy, his heavy sac slapping against her skin. His hips thrust against her bottom, lifting her up onto her toes. Charlotte bore down to take him deep inside. It was his turn to groan. She clamped her muscles tight around his cock, slowing his movements.

"Charlotte, if you do that again, I will spill." His voice was strained.

She smiled, considering it for a moment, then squeezed. Ahmose gripped her tighter and then thrust one more time, a cry dying on his lips. His hips continued to flex and move. She could feel his hot seed spurting into her body, filling her womb. For a moment the thought panicked her, but then Charlotte realized if she got pregnant, it would be okay because she'd be carrying Ahmose's child.

"You are truly a sorceress, my love." He dragged in a ragged breath. "And I thank the gods that you are mine."

Charlotte rested her head on the bed. She wasn't sure if when she moved, her legs would support her. Sweat dripped down her back and under her breasts. Her pussy lips felt pouty and swollen. The room smelled of spice and sex…their sex. Their lovemaking was the sweetest aroma she'd ever inhaled.

Ahmose lifted her from behind and placed her on the bed. He gathered the rumpled covers before slipping in beside her and pulling Charlotte tight against his smooth chest.

Chapter Four

The next day Ahmose had the chariot waiting. They were off to the city of Gurob to the harem palace.

The ride through the countryside was breathtaking—fertile fields, the Nile in the distance. Charlotte closed her eyes for a moment trying to store the picture in her mind for eternity. The air was clean and lightly scented with flowers.

Ahmose led her past several temples on the journey to middle Egypt, each one more spectacular than the last. He pointed out the fact that most were still under construction and would continue to be for years to come, because honoring the gods took time. Charlotte wished she could tell him that these temples would be much loved for thousands of years.

They arrived at the harem palace a couple hours later. Ahmose had stopped along the way to greet the people, taking time to enter fields and help out where needed. From what Charlotte could see he was well liked and well respected by all, winning over everyone who crossed his path. *No wonder you were able to unite the kingdoms of Egypt.* Her admiration and love for him grew stronger by the minute.

* * * * *

The palace was smaller than the one he lived in at Thebes, but far homier. Trees from the nearby oasis flourished, their thick, dense leaves shading much of the dwelling. Plump dates were cultivated in the fields, giving the air a sweet, fruity aroma. Grass the color of emeralds grew abundant enough to allow Hasani to graze.

A beautiful woman greeted them at the door, her skin the color of roasted almonds, and a regal countenance that was born, not learned. Her eyes were the same black fire as Ahmose's. She wore a perfectly braided ebony wig and immaculate white linens draped over her pert nipples and lithe form. Jealousy streaked through Charlotte and her stomach knotted as she pictured Ahmose sinking his cock into this beautiful woman's cunt. His head buried between the woman's spread thighs lapping at her plump folds until she screamed out an earth shattering release. Charlotte fisted her hands.

"King Kamose is not here. He is visiting his fields."

Ahmose nodded, kissed the woman on the cheek, then immediately pulled Charlotte forward. "I'd like you to meet my mother, Ashotep."

The woman smiled and rushed forward to embrace her, pushing Ahmose to the side. Charlotte's discomfort faded instantly, replaced by embarrassment. And to think she'd actually considered throttling the woman. Ashotep tugged Charlotte's hands, hurrying her inside, and out of the hot midday sun.

"Ahmose sent word that his chosen one had arrived, but I did not believe it until I saw you with my own eyes," his mother said, her smile growing.

She wasn't quite sure how to respond to what Ashotep had just told her. When had Ahmose found time to send a message?

"It is not everyday that a son brings home his future bride," Ashotep continued, her voice rising with excitement.

She glanced over her shoulder at Ahmose, her eyes narrowing. He raised his eyebrows in innocence. "It's very nice to meet you." She squeezed the woman's hands before releasing them.

Charlotte tried to imagine her mother in the same position. Would Victoria enthusiastically welcome Ahmose as her soon to be son-in-law? She doubted it. Not unless he came with a pile of ancient gold relics and the keys to Egypt.

Ashotep's smile deepened. "We will break bread and then you can tell us about you. There is much to prepare in such a short time."

Charlotte's brows furrowed.

"You must be excited about your wedding," Ashotep gushed.

Charlotte's stomach twisted, forming a bundle of nerves. Could she really go through with this? As much as she'd like to spend her life with Ahmose, she would feel guilty leaving her parents without a word. *If she could even return to her own time...*

The conversation was lively as they dined. Ahmose's mother told tales of the trouble he used to get into when he was a little boy. Charlotte glanced at him from beneath her lashes. It wasn't hard to imagine Ahmose as a little boy with those big black eyes and ebony hair. He probably charmed his way out of getting punished. His children would be exact copies of him. Her heart squeezed in her chest at the thought of Ahmose with kids.

He would be a good father, patient and loving, yet firm. She swallowed the bread she'd been chewing, and it lodged in her throat. It wouldn't do to think about such things. Once she was gone, he'd move on, find himself an Egyptian bride and go on to rule Egypt. Logically Charlotte knew that was the way things should happen, but no matter how many times she tried to convince herself, she still couldn't picture Ahmose with anyone but her. The thought of another woman wrapping her body around him nauseated her.

A few hours later, they said their goodbyes. Ashotep promised to help with the wedding plans and assured Charlotte she was marrying a prince of a man. No one had to convince Charlotte. Ahmose was everything she could ever want in a husband. He'd had her at the first glance.

They rode back to the palace in Thebes as the sun lowered on the horizon. The sounds of families in their homes wafted into the streets, their voices rising high with laughter. Spice filled the air as the various kitchens were put to good use.

"What are you thinking?" Ahmose whispered near her ear.

"I'm thinking how wonderful a place Egypt is and how great the people are." She smiled to herself.

A land she'd helped uncover from the sands of time now rose proudly before her like a sentinel standing guard at the gates of heaven. If she did end up returning to her own time, no one would believe the tale she'd tell, certainly not her parents. Charlotte knew without a doubt she'd never be able to breathe a word without fear of being locked away.

* * * * *

That evening Ahmose was especially romantic in his lovemaking. He anointed her body with myrrh-scented oil, pouring it from a Syrian-inspired vessel. His hands were gentle as he smoothed the liquid over her shoulders and down her arms, carefully avoiding her beaded nipples and aching clitoris. He rubbed oil into her legs and over her buttocks, kneading them firmly as he made his way up her back. Ahmose rubbed until the last of the kinks were gone.

She was practically swaying with need when his palms finally made contact with her nipples. He brushed the pads of his thumbs over the rose-tipped peaks and they grew rigid with desire. Her breathing came out in ragged gasps. He continued to play with her full mounds, molding and shaping.

Charlotte's channel flooded and she mewed. She shifted to stave off the ache. It only added to the friction. When Ahmose leaned down and whisked his tongue across her stiff crests, she almost came.

He suckled her tortured peak, tugging with his lips, then his teeth. When she thought she could stand no more Ahmose switched to her other nipple. He fed hungrily, flicking his tongue, capturing it again and again as if this were the last time they'd get to lie together. She moaned. He pushed her back toward the bed without breaking contact. Her nipples were engorged by the time he'd settled her on the edge of the reed mat.

Charlotte's breathing was choppy at best. Her breasts throbbed and tingled as heat raced over her oiled skin, centering at the juncture between her spread thighs. Ahmose dropped to his knees before her, then slipped his hands behind her and pulled her forward until her pussy was level with his mouth. He glanced up from beneath long lashes and smiled. The act was simply carnal, telling Charlotte without words that he was about to eat her alive. Her clitoris pulsed.

Ahmose leaned forward and inhaled. "Your scent drives me wild. I feel like an animal when you are near."

Dew dripped down the soft curls between Charlotte's spread legs, inviting him to drink deep. She smelled musky and aroused, the oil of myrrh only adding to her allure. She bit her lip as he dipped his head closer and gently blew warm air on her heated flesh. Charlotte shivered, her nipples jutting out like ripe fruit fresh for the picking. Ahmose lifted one leg and slipped it over his shoulder, then repeated the action with her other, tipping her cunny toward his face.

"Do you know how much I long to taste you and touch you?" he growled in the back of his throat. "You are so beautiful, I'm surprised Ra has not come to claim you for himself."

He smiled again, letting Charlotte see the fire that she'd ignited inside him, the passion that burned unending; the need that screamed out from his cock, and the love that he felt in his heart. She was his and he was hers. That was how it was and how it should be.

Ahmose leaned forward and swiped his tongue over her swollen lips. Charlotte shuddered and closed her eyes. He could feel her body's tension, the underlying desperation, and the overall yearning hidden deep inside.

"Food shall never taste the same to me from this day forth. For it could never compare to the bounty between your thighs."

He laved her again, circling her hot wet sheath, teasing her pussy with his tongue. Her tender flesh responded by dampening more and puffing out. Ahmose, intoxicated by her scent, swayed drunkenly with her responsiveness. He dove in, uncovering the hidden jewel lying beneath her heated folds.

Charlotte's nails bit into his shoulders as he sucked the bud into his mouth and gently worried it with his teeth. She gasped, unable to catch her breath.

"Ahmose…" She groaned.

He circled her clitoris with his tongue, sliding it back and forth in imitation of a snake. It was all it took to send her over the edge.

"I'm coming…"

Her channel flooded, wetting his chin, and still Ahmose fed, lapping up every last drop of her release.

Charlotte threw her head back and screamed. Her body convulsed as her orgasm slammed down upon her. Ahmose's face lay buried between her legs, devouring her. She couldn't seem to control the shudders racking her body. Her vision faded to black and she blinked to gain back her senses. Her skin was alive and pulsing as contraction after contraction rocked her.

She lay back on the bed waiting for her breathing to return to normal. Ahmose stayed between her legs, placing tender kisses upon her thighs. It took several minutes before Charlotte could piece together a coherent sentence. When she did, she sat up on her elbows and kept it short.

"My turn," she purred, licking her lips and pulling him up onto the bed beside her.

Ahmose lay on his back, his arms covering his eyes. His cock was hard enough to pound gold. He didn't think he'd ever tire of feeding from Charlotte's endless well. She was ambrosia, sweeter than the finest wines in Egypt and more precious than all his gold and gems combined. Her taste simmered in his mouth, tempting his appetite. Her breathing had finally slowed to a satisfied purr. Ahmose contented himself with the fact that he'd been able to please her as no other.

He grinned and was just about to turn to tell her when he felt her lips slip over the crown of his cock. The air seemed to freeze in his lungs. Unable to gasp or speak, he waited. Her touch was tentative at first, a quick lick followed by a gentle suck. Ahmose held as still as the dead, forcing himself to keep from thrusting. When he was finally able to draw air it was on a gasp.

"Does that feel all right?" Her voice quavered as she spoke around his cock.

Ahmose uncovered his eyes and looked down at her. "It feels like a thousand tiny butterflies have alighted on my staff."

Charlotte licked him from balls to tip and back again. "Do you like it when I suck you?"

Ahmose groaned. "You have no idea."

She took him into her mouth and began to suck. Ahmose's muscles tightened and he gripped the sheets. She swirled her tongue over the sensitive head, sliding it around his length. The pressure of her mouth increased, coinciding with the building pressure inside Ahmose. He felt his sac rise, drawing near his body, ready for release.

Charlotte's fingers slipped around the base of his cock and she began matching rhythm with her mouth. The combination of her wetness with the silky smoothness of her skin was too much for him.

"You must stop," he gritted out between clenched teeth.

She shook her head without breaking stride, increasing the speed of her motions.

"I can't hold back." He gasped, the muscles in his abdomen contracting.

"Mmm," she purred over his cock.

Ahmose almost came off the bed. He grasped her silky hair, at the same time thrusting up into her molten mouth. The searing heat combined with the pressure from her sucking sent shockwaves through his body. His cock rejoiced. He jerked and thrust once more, then sent his seed jettisoning out into her mouth and down her throat. Charlotte didn't try to pull back. Instead she drank deep. Ahmose trembled and quaked, his body exhausted.

He pulled Charlotte up beside him. "You are amazing."

She blushed. "Do you really think so?"

He brushed a wisp of hair off her face and kissed her. "I know so."

* * * * *

The days passed quickly, leading up to the Opet festival, where the pharaoh would be reborn. The celebration would also signal the return of Sopdet, a bright star on the horizon, marking the Egyptian New Year.

Charlotte's wedding day had arrived. So blissfully in love, she'd decided even if the opportunity to return to her own time should appear, she would not take it. Her life, her heart, and her future happiness were here with Ahmose.

Her soon to be husband had given her token gifts of his affection every day since she'd arrived. His lavish presents, like his love, were endless. Ahmose asked for nothing in exchange. Yet Charlotte couldn't assuage the guilt she felt about not being able to gift him back. She knew that the act of giving presents was a large part of the marriage ceremony. She ran her hand over the Tears of Amun and a chill skittered over her. She quickly dismissed the feeling as wedding jitters.

The city of Thebes was abuzz about the festival. Preparations had begun early in the week and were now culminating. Tonight, the people of Egypt would gather at the temple of Karnak, bringing out Amun, his wife Mut, and their son Khonsu's statues on sacred barques. They'd then be carried in procession along the sphinx-lined route that connected Karnak to Luxor. Worshipers believed that at the Luxor temple, in the inner sanctuary, Amun would ritually unite with Ahmose's mother so that she could again give birth to the royal *Ka*.

When the ceremony ended King Kamose would enter the sanctuary, merging with his newborn *Ka*. He would later reappear, replenished with divine power, as the son of Amun-Ra. King Kamose would then receive the crowds. Dancers would perform and great offerings of meat and bread would be made. Once presented and ultimately enjoyed by the gods, the bounty would be distributed to the people.

Charlotte was excited about the celebration, but dread had settled into her bones like an anchor, pulling her down despite her enthusiasm. Ashotep had brought a special gown from Gurob with her and had fashioned an elegant wig for Charlotte's head. She assured Charlotte that she looked beautiful, and then escorted her to the courtyard of the palace where Ahmose was waiting.

Charlotte's breath caught when she spotted Ahmose. So handsome, so regal. He stood, loose-limbed, near a fig tree with a small crown of gold on his wigged head. Ahmose wore a fresh, embroidered kilt that had been fashioned and inlayed with precious gems. A scarab of gold graced his ring finger. His hands were at his sides. Despite his relaxed appearance, his shoulders looked tense. His eyes sought hers, holding, confirming she was truly there, and only then did he appear to relax.

The ceremony, which amounted to little more than holding hands and declaring one's intentions, was over within minutes. By the time they'd finished, Charlotte's head was swimming. She didn't know if it was fear or exhilaration. Either way, it was over and nothing would come between them. Charlotte turned to her husband and placed a chaste kiss upon his lips.

"Remember always, I love you."

Ahmose's fingers trembled as he brought them to her face. "You have nothing to fear now. It is done."

Charlotte breathed a sigh of relief, trying to ignore the lingering dread, lurking like a shadow in the back of her mind. It seemed to be growing in intensity, like a storm on the horizon, moving swiftly, decimating everything in its path. Charlotte pushed it aside and smiled at Ahmose. *It's just wedding jitters.* They would eventually die down and she'd forget about them, so they could enjoy the Opet festival tonight.

Ashotep left to prepare herself for her part in the rituals. Ahmose pulled Charlotte into his arms and kissed her deeply. "You are now mine—all mine and no one can take you away," he whispered against her lips, rocking her from side to side. Eventually his head came to rest on top of hers.

Charlotte could feel the tension in his muscles. "You feel it too, don't you?"

His muscles locked, holding her tight. "I feel nothing but happiness on this day."

Despite his words of assurance, Charlotte sensed that he seemed reluctant to release her.

Chapter Five

The festival was a joyous occasion. Charlotte joined Ahmose and his family in the royal entourage as they made their way from Karnak to Luxor temple. The mood was jubilant, yet sedated. It should have been the happiest day of her life, but she couldn't seem to bring herself to celebrate. Ahmose strolled silently beside her, his hand holding her own. Strength poured off him in waves as he silently sent her reassurances.

Charlotte stayed close, afraid to release him for fear her dream would fade away. Which was ridiculous—she'd already been here for nearly a week. She'd found no way back in that time, nor desired to return.

The crowd gathered outside the temple, their hushed voices chanting in unison. Ahmose's mother had been inside the sanctuary for several hours by now, convening with the gods. His brother, King Kamose, stepped forward and entered the temple.

The full moon glowed yellow in the sky, its shimmering light abundant, making the use of torches all but unnecessary. An hour later King Kamose emerged, vibrant. The crowd broke out of their reverie, cheering and rushing forward quickly to make their offerings.

With the gods appeased, the mood turned outright hedonistic. Wine flowed freely, along with barley beer. Platters of bread, fish, gazelle, and geese were passed around for everyone to sample. Ahmose gathered food for them, then pulled Charlotte away from the crowd.

He stuck his mouth next to her left ear. "I'm selfish. I want you to myself."

They strolled back toward the temple of Karnak, passing revelers along the way. The moonlight glistened upon the waters of the Nile. In the distance, clouds gathered on the horizon, heralding an incoming storm. The breeze picked up, carrying perfumed oils and cypress grass in its wake. Hand-in-hand they walked back. Ahmose took Charlotte around the temple until they were standing next to the sacred lake.

"I wanted to return to the place where I first laid eyes on you, so that I can offer the gods my thanks." He spoke low and deep as he pulled her back against his chest, his arms wrapping around her waist.

Charlotte shivered as a raindrop spattered her face. "This place will always hold fond memories for me, also." She squeezed his hands. "It's where I met the man I've loved for as long as I can remember."

She didn't have to see his frown to feel it. The tension in his body increased tenfold. "How could you have loved me for years, when I just met you a few sunrises ago?"

Charlotte turned in his arms until she faced him. The moon was so bright she could easily make out his features, even with clouds closing in. "What is important is that we've found each other and we're in love." She framed his face with her hands and rose up on tiptoe to kiss him once more.

"You are my love," he said when she pulled back. "My only love."

Charlotte bit her lip and then smiled. "There's something I want to give you."

Ahmose stilled her hands as she moved toward her neck. "That is not necessary, Charlotte. You are gift enough." He lifted her chin and began to nibble on her lips.

"I can't think when you do that, you know."

He laughed. "That is the purpose."

"Ahmose…" He continued to feast upon her mouth. "Ahmose, please."

He stilled. Lightning flashed in the distance, followed by a loud crack of thunder. Charlotte looked warily at the incoming storm before turning back to Ahmose.

"You've given me so much. I want to show you how much you mean to me."

He frowned for a moment and then sighed. "If that is what you wish, I will accept your gift."

Charlotte reached for the clasp on the Tears of Amun. It seemed to catch for a moment before slipping free. Ahmose turned and allowed her to put it on him. The air around them turned electric.

Facing her once again, he asked, "What do you think? I'm sure it looks better upon you."

Charlotte smiled, as a wave of dizziness washed over her. "I lov—aahhh!" The scream ripped from her insides.

Pain shot through her and she couldn't seem to focus, as if a spike were being driven through her skull. Rain started to fall in sheets. Charlotte could see Ahmose's lips moving, his eyes rounded in fear. He struggled to grasp hold of her, but couldn't seem to do so. Her gold wedding ring dropped from her hand. The storm raged around them. His handsome face swam before her eyes. One minute he was there.

The next he was gone.

"Noooo…" Charlotte cried out, but it was too late. Lightning flashed nearby, rattling her teeth. She was falling. Falling back toward the water. Back into the sacred lake. "Ahmose, I love you," she shouted one more time, praying that her words reached him.

* * * * *

Charlotte broke the water's surface, sputtering, her mouth full of moss. The sun was shining brightly and it took a few seconds before she was actually able to see. Her hair was plastered to her head, sans the wig she'd been wearing. She knew without looking that Ahmose was not with her. She wiped her face and pulled herself from the water. Her heart and body ached as if she were being torn asunder.

"Where have you been, young lady?" a shrill voice behind her asked.

Charlotte closed her eyes and took a deep breath before turning to face her mother. The sun was shining brightly, heating the air to oven temperatures. Her heart ached to the point of bursting.

"What did you do to your dress?" The frown on her mother's face would have wilted flowers and seemed to be deepening by the second. "What on earth are you wearing? It's positively scandalous."

Charlotte glanced down and vaguely registered the fact she was still wearing her Egyptian kilt. Her body was unadorned of jewelry; it seemed the precious metal could not survive time-travel. *Except the Tears of Amun.*

"I'm glad we decided to come looking for you when you didn't show up to help. Goodness knows what we would have found had we not."

Charlotte's brows knitted. "What do you mean?"

"Don't play dimwitted with me, Charlotte Constance Witherspoon." Her mother stepped forward then stopped, her eyes narrowing on the front of Charlotte's wrap.

Charlotte glanced down and gasped. Her shirt had once again gone sheer, except this time she wore nothing underneath to disguise her nakedness. The sound of heavy feet caught her attention. Field workers rushed forward, their harried voices growing louder as they approached.

"Goodness..." Her mother sucked in a surprised breath as she glanced over her shoulder. "Henry, get down here this instant! And for heaven's sake lend us your outer shirt. *Your* daughter is dressed like a...like a...harlot!" Victoria snapped her fingers and Henry jumped, ambling forward.

"I daresay, what have you gotten up to, gel?" he asked, handing over his shirt to Charlotte, his jowled features reddening beneath his hat.

Victoria harrumphed. "I know what it looks like she's been doing." She arched a fine brow, not bothering to lower her voice. Victoria pulled a handkerchief from her sleeve, bringing it to her mouth to cover her disdain.

Charlotte gazed at the crowd of workers whispering to each other, their eyes as round as saucers. Slowly she reached for the shirt her father had offered, wrapping it around her. Shivers wracked her body. "I'm sorry, Papa." She glanced down, unable to meet his eyes.

Henry's eyes softened for a moment, then he coughed. "Don't want to hear it. Don't want to hear it." His hand was waving away any chance Charlotte would be given to explain. "Can't tell you how disappointed I am."

Explain…how in the world could she do that, when she didn't even understand what had happened?

Her full week of love and happiness had passed in mere hours here. Charlotte grabbed her aching head. Her world had tilted upside down and she'd landed on the wrong side. The Tears of Amun were gone, lost in time. Since she'd placed them about Ahmose's neck there was no chance of getting them back. The pain from that realization struck deep. Charlotte began to sob.

She was well and truly stuck here.

* * * * *

Her days passed in a blur. Life with her parents had resumed a normal pace, with one exception. Charlotte was no longer allowed to travel alone without their escort. The pain Charlotte had felt upon realizing there would be no returning to her true love had turned into a dull, continuous ache. Her eyes were a permanent shade of red and the puffiness refused to go down. Of course, it didn't help that she couldn't seem to stop crying. Charlotte was convinced she'd shed enough tears to flood the Nile Valley.

She thought about Ahmose. Twelve long days had passed since she'd last laid eyes on him. In his world she'd been gone nearly three months. Had he given up on finding her? Had he already forgotten about her? Was he waiting for her to return? Had he found someone new? The last thought had her heart tripping in her chest.

Back in her own world Charlotte couldn't seem to find her feet. She'd gone through the motions at the dinner parties she'd attended with her parents. She played the doting daughter part to the teeth. All the while her stomach churned with unease. Charlotte hadn't seemed to be able to keep any food down since returning.

Tonight she was being dragged to another boring affair. Lady Alexandra Stuart had invited them to dinner, which in Victoria's eye was a big coup. Charlotte's mother had been especially diligent in watching her prepare for the evening, even going as far as to pick out a dress for her to wear. But Charlotte couldn't summon the energy to care.

* * * * *

Dinner turned out to be positively dreadful. Victoria had hoped to set her up with Lady Alexandria Stuart's son. Charlotte cringed as she recalled Robert's clammy fingers upon her hand. Raw liver was more appealing. Ahmose's touch had been so warm, firm, and gentle by comparison. Charlotte dismissed Robert unceremoniously.

By the time the evening closed and they'd reached their Model T, Victoria was fuming. "Why don't you want to see him?"

Because his touch doesn't set me aflame, make my nipples ache, my pussy throb.

"He's unsuitable, Mother. And he feels the same about me, I assure you."

Victoria gaze leveled. "You must have misunderstood him. Robert is from good stock, quite good blood. He wouldn't think such a thing."

"Believe what you want, Mother." Charlotte didn't bother to hide the exasperation in her voice.

Victoria's features hardened. "It's no wonder he thinks such things with the fodder going about town. Your virtue is in question."

Charlotte laughed; she couldn't help it. Her virtue was long gone. She pictured Ahmose above her, driving his thick cock inside her willing body. Charlotte knew she'd done nothing wrong, but still the guilt over dragging her family name through the muck pervaded. She considered apologizing, when her stomach suddenly rolled and lurched.

"Pull over please," she begged in desperation.

"We shall not," her mother vetoed.

Charlotte gripped the door. "I'm going to be ill." She threw the door open and leaned her head out in time to lose the entire contents of her stomach.

Afterwards, Charlotte slumped back down on the seat, staring out into the night.

"Gracious, Charlotte, what is the matter with you?" Victoria grabbed her kerchief and held it to her nose in disgust. "I believe I'll send a call out to Dr. Williams tomorrow."

"No!" Charlotte sprang to life. She had a pretty good idea what was wrong with her and she didn't need Dr. Williams confirming it. Things were bad enough between her and her parents. They didn't need to know she was carrying a two-thousand-year-old pharaoh's baby. She pulled herself together enough to look her mother in the eye. "I mean that won't be necessary mother. I'm feeling much better at the present. I believe I've just caught a bug."

Victoria eyed her suspiciously.

"Oh for Pete's sake, Victoria, leave her be," Henry grumbled.

Charlotte smiled tentatively at her father. He winked at her and then looked forward as if nothing had occurred.

Chapter Six

The next day Charlotte rose early, forcing herself to keep down some toast. Her menses had not arrived, confirming her worst fear and her greatest hope…she was pregnant. Somehow, despite the circumstances and against all odds, Ahmose and she were going to have a baby. Charlotte was overjoyed that a piece of him still existed within her yet terrified of her parent's reaction.

Charlotte frowned, unable to come up with a solution to the latter problem.

Her attention turned back to Ahmose and the life she had growing inside her. She placed her hand on her stomach. The thought of Ahmose not getting to see his child brought fresh tears to her eyes. It wasn't fair. Their love was not supposed to end this way. She pictured his face. The sadness she'd been feeling returned with a vengeance. Charlotte swallowed hard.

"I've got to be strong for you," she spoke, rubbing her belly.

An hour or so later her parents filed into the room. Her mother and father were setting off for the Cairo museum as soon as they broke their fast.

"Get your things together Charlotte, you're coming with us," Victoria stated between bites of toast and sips of tea.

"Mother…" Charlotte hesitated. "I thought perhaps I could stay home today and catch up on my studies."

Victoria stopped mid-bite and stared at her. She glanced at Charlotte's plate then back at her face. "You've eaten, so you obviously feel better. It would do you well, under the circumstances, to get some air." Victoria paused, her eyes narrowing. "Unless you aren't feeling better, in which case, I'll call for Dr. Williams."

Charlotte glanced at her plate then back up into her mother's face. There was no use arguing. "I'm feeling better," she lied.

"Well then, it's settled. Get yourself ready, we'll be leaving within an hour." Victoria dabbed her napkin at the corners of her mouth. "Besides, you'll learn a great deal more at the museum than you will in one of those books. Right, Henry?"

Her father coughed, his bushy brows rising as if trying to figure out what had been said. He looked at Charlotte and then at his wife. Charlotte followed his gaze. Her mother's frown said it all.

"Right," he blustered.

Charlotte rose from the table and went to her room to change. They were out of the house within an hour and on their way. The ride into Cairo was dusty as usual. She and her mother had to hang onto their hats as the wind picked up speed. The invisible breeze carried the odor of spice-filled cooking on its wings, triggering Charlotte's memory. She blushed as she recalled the last time she'd encountered that particular aroma. Ahmose had been standing behind her in the chariot, his hard cock filling her greedy pussy as they road through the streets of Thebes. The bumps had driven him deep inside her body until he'd actually nudged her womb. Had that been when she'd gotten pregnant?

Charlotte crossed her legs, trying to assuage the familiar ache that had begun. She missed his muscled body rising above her, his hairless chest scraping her engorged nipples, and his hips as they pistoned, sending his cock in and out of her moist sheath. Tears filled her eyes at the thought of never getting to experience those sensations again with Ahmose. They'd been so new and wonderful; she couldn't imagine life without them. At the same time, sharing her body with anyone else was out of the question. The thought was repulsive. His touch and his touch alone was what she sought.

The sky was clear and blue with the exception of a dark cloud lingering on the horizon. Since it was the flooding season that wasn't particularly unusual. By the time they arrived at the museum they were all covered in dust. Charlotte patted down her skirt and shook out her hat. She glanced at the horizon once more. The dark cloud had shifted, drawing nearer, instead of farther away. Charlotte placed her hat back on her head, instantly shading her eyes. The spot in the distance shouldn't have gotten any closer given its position when they left. She fought back a shiver, then turned her eyes away.

It's just a storm. Shivers racked her body as memories from a similar storm filled her mind. *Stop being silly.* Charlotte wiped away the gooseflesh rising on her arms and followed her parents into the museum. Past the entrance, the museum opened into a wider space. Tutankhamen had already been situated in his own private area with more objects added daily as they uncovered them.

"Come, Charlotte," her mother called out, turning toward Tut's gold.

Charlotte walked a few steps behind, her eyes fixing on several familiar items. Ahmose had owned jars like the ones she was viewing, their vibrant colors and designs still breathtaking after all those years in the ground. Charlotte longed to run her hands over the pottery and combs, anything to make herself feel closer to Ahmose and the world she'd lost.

A tug at her hand snapped her attention back.

"Really, Charlotte, must I hold your hand to get you to follow?" Her mother gazed at her, shaking her head. "I'm about ready to give up. Perhaps you should go stay with Aunt Edna in Surrey, if you're so unhappy here."

"No! I mean, no, I love Egypt. It's my home." Charlotte squeezed her mother's hand, willing her to understand.

For a moment Victoria's features softened, then just as quickly the hard mask returned. "Well then, come on." She pulled, dragging Charlotte behind.

They finished examining Howard Carter's find and then headed into the other rooms. They were less organized, a mismatch of Egyptian artifacts, some labeled, others not. The museum was still in its growing stage, and as such was still finding its feet in the world. Several of the displays were set up to depict tombs. Charlotte walked by each one, reading the markers beneath.Guards stood at the entrances of each room, their brown, mustached faces grim, ensuring no one stole any of the items. Punishment in Egypt was harsh. Just last week a man's hand was cut off for stealing coins from a wealthy sheik. The practice was positively barbaric, but served as a good deterrent to crime.

Her mother had considered protesting the Egyptian government, only to be stopped by her father. Charlotte grinned as she remembered that moment. It was the only time she could recall where her mother actually conceded to her father. A victory she knew her father would cherish for life.

Wandering without looking where she was going, Charlotte found herself in a smaller room. The air inside this area was still and musty, as if no one really came in here all that much. She glanced up. Her parents were nowhere in sight. Her mother would not be happy once she noticed Charlotte's absence. A boom sounded above the displays. The guards in the doorways glanced at each other and shifted uneasily.

Charlotte gazed around trying to place the sound. Another loud crack shattered the quiet. Hair on her arms stood on end. She stared out toward a blocked area that had earlier reflected sunlight. It now lay in shadows. Obviously the storm she'd seen on the horizon had caught up with them.

Charlotte ignored the tension in her shoulders and continued on. She glanced at several rows of papyrus, reading the stories they told. Her mind drifted back to ancient times. The peoples smiling faces, the simple joy their lives held. She closed her eyes, banishing the glorious thoughts from her head.

Whack!

Charlotte jumped as lightning struck nearby, shaking the columns in the building. One of the guards had caught her movement and now was following her with his eyes. She turned away, trying to ignore him. Her mother's voice rang out as her parents entered the room next to the one she was standing in.

"Have you seen a young lady with brown, curly hair, about so tall?"

Charlotte spun in time to see her mother interrogating the guard who'd been watching her. He slowly raised his hand and extended his finger in her direction. Charlotte harrumphed. So much for a few moments of peace. Her mother was marching toward her with Henry in tow. When she reached Charlotte, she halted.

"I thought I told you to stay with us."

"You did, Mother. I didn't realize you weren't here until just minutes ago." Charlotte kept her voice level. The sound carried easily inside the museum, much like when you were in a tomb.

"So your father and I are so insignificant that you don't notice whether we are here or not." Victoria placed her hands on her hips. Her raised voice had further caught the attention of the guards. The one who'd been watching Charlotte earlier was now moving closer.

"Of course not, Mother," Charlotte whispered, glancing over her mother's shoulder at the curious guard.

Victoria followed her gaze. Charlotte saw the guard's steps falter.

"Now where were we?" her mother asked, knowing perfectly well where they'd left off. "My mind is made up, Charlotte. I've spoken with your father and he thinks it's a good idea also. Right Henry?"

"Right, right," her father added before looking away, unable to meet Charlotte's questioning gaze.

"What's a good idea?" A lump had formed in Charlotte's throat as she forced the words out.

"You're going to stay with Aunt Edna just as soon as we can book you passage."

"But Mother, we had this discussion moments ago." Charlotte choked as sorrow leapt inside of her, wrapping itself around her throat until she was unable to breathe. Her mother didn't understand what she was asking of her.

Victoria snorted. "I've changed my mind."

Cold swept through her, like the jagged edge of a knife being plunged into her heart. "Mind…changed…but you can't. I told you how much I love it here," she pleaded.

"Don't cause a scene," Victoria hissed, glancing back toward the guard. "I know what you said earlier, but Egypt really isn't the proper place for a young lady. I was wrong to bring you here."

The finality in her mother's words slammed like a steel trap in Charlotte's mind. How could she think that bringing her to Egypt had been wrong? Everything good that had ever happened to her had occurred here, in this land. Charlotte didn't have any idea what she would do with herself back in London. The place seemed cold to her, unwelcoming. The rain that fell there blanketed the city in a wall of never-ending gray. She trembled even thinking about it.

"Now finish up in here, so we can be on our way." Victoria gathered her skirts and turned toward the door. Henry followed. Instead of continuing further, she halted, waiting for Charlotte.

Charlotte's stomach clenched. She felt as if she'd been struck by a blow. The storm raged on outside, while the storm inside her had already blown over. There was nothing left to say. Her mother had made up her mind. She would be packed up and carted off to London within a few days. What about Egypt? What about Ahmose? She couldn't bear to be that far away from either of them. Charlotte wasn't sure what she was going to do.

Her eyes gazed unseeing at the displays before her, as she made her way around the room. Tears pooled, threatening to spill. She was about to turn and join her parents when a sarcophagus in a corner caught her attention. She glanced over her shoulder. Her parents were still standing in the doorway, but now they were conversing with the guard. His black eyes, so much like Ahmose's, kept watching her.

Charlotte turned back to gaze at the sarcophagus. Glass surrounded it like a cage. The skin on her scalp tightened. There was no name on the plate, only information stating the Egyptologists believed the man in the case to be royalty, perhaps even a pharaoh, and had been found in Deir el-Bahari cache.

According to cartouches found with the body, he'd never married after his love vanished near the sacred waters of Karnak. Her chest tensed as the implications sunk into her mind. She stared unbelieving as her lungs labored for air. Charlotte's gaze ran from the mummy's feet, up his legs, over his shriveled waist, stopping at his chest. Her vision, blurred by the unshed tears, refused to clear. She took a ragged breath and wiped at her eyes. Charlotte blinked.

It couldn't be. No way. *Was it? Please…*

Like a brilliant rainbow of gold, the Tears of Amun shone through the dim lighting, drawing her near. Charlotte's heart slammed against her ribs. Her gaze flew to the mummy's face…sightless eyes stared back. It was Ahmose. Searing pain stabbed at her heart, ripping away the last shreds of her sanity. Her head began to spin. What was she going to do? She glanced at her parents who were now looking her way. Her mother grabbed her father's pocket watch and tapped it impatiently. Charlotte heaved air into her lungs. Her mind was racing a mile a minute.

If it worked once, would it work again? She had no way of knowing. *And what if placing the Tears of Amun around her neck didn't work?* Charlotte had no doubt she'd be arrested. They'd probably chop off her hand, and quite possibly sentence her to death considering who she would be committing the crime against. But if she didn't try she'd find herself back in London with her Aunt Edna, raising her baby alone.

Charlotte stared at her necklace, her muscles locked in place. She heard the tap of her mother's foot as her patience reached its end. Within seconds her mother would come for her and then it would be all over. Charlotte took a step forward, her mind made up. She'd rather suffer the consequences than live her life looking back and wondering "what if." Without further thought, her eyes firmly on the target, Charlotte raised her fist and smashed the glass, cutting her hand in the process.

Blood dripped onto the floor like crimson teardrops.

Her hands closed over the necklace. Slipping the clasp, she pulled it away from Ahmose. In the distance Charlotte heard her mother scream. There was a lot of shuffling of feet, but it all appeared muffled over the sound of her heartbeat. She placed the Tears of Amun on, the gold once again heavy around her neck. The air crackled as thunder burst in the sky. Charlotte turned, gazing at the scene before her.

Her father was struggling to keep the guard from rushing toward her, while her mother's hands were pressed against her cheeks in a frozen mask of outrage. Their raised voices didn't seem to reach her ears as

Charlotte stared on, waiting for something to happen. The guard finally freed himself from her father's grip and rushed forward.

Nothing was happening. She was about to be arrested for stealing from the Egyptian Museum and there was absolutely nothing she could do about it.

"Sorry, Papa...I love you," Charlotte cried out to her father, who was staring at her, agog. The guard's movements seemed to slow until he appeared to be moving in reverse. Charlotte stared in fascination as he swept past her parents. The world seemed to tip on its axis and then Charlotte was falling...falling...

* * * * *

Charlotte took a deep breath and opened her eyes. She blinked twice, unable to trust her vision. She opened them again and sure enough, Ahmose's smiling face was leaning over her.

"I thought I'd lost you forever," he murmured, his voice full of pain and joy all at once.

Charlotte smiled and glanced around. She was in his palace in Thebes. "How did I get here?" she croaked, her throat parched as if she'd been lying there for days.

"You were found in Cairo by one of my servants." He brought a cup to her lips, bidding her to drink. "When you disappeared I sent everyone who could be spared out to find you." He swallowed, his black eyes misting up. "I had almost given up hope."

"Me too," she choked. "We should have remembered the inscription on the box. If we had we would never have doubted that we would be together again."

He laughed and kissed her. "Perhaps you are right. I should have recalled a fated love that must once again be." He pressed his lips to hers again, igniting the fire within her.

Charlotte gripped his shoulders, pulling him closer until his chest made contact with her aching breasts. She moaned, unable to get enough of his heat. Ahmose deepened the kiss. She slipped her hand under his kilt and began stroking his cock, reveling in the feel of his satiny hardness. His fingers tangled in her hair as he savaged her mouth. All the frustration and fear had culminated to this one moment. They needed to feel each other physically, to prove that this was real.

Charlotte grasped the belt at Ahmose's waist and tugged, while her other hand continued to pleasure him. The kilt fell to the floor.

Ahmose grabbed the linen covering her and yanked it away, revealing Charlotte's naked splendor. He released her lips and pulled away from her long enough to drink his fill, before tracing the ridges around her engorged nipples. They pebbled against his palm.

"In all the lands of Egypt, there is no beauty such as yours." His voice was hoarse, as he choked back emotion.

"Come," she said breathlessly. "Show me."

Ahmose didn't hesitate. He slipped between Charlotte's thighs, his cock sliding over her damp pussy. He closed his eyes and groaned. "I fear I cannot wait a moment longer, my love. I must be inside you."

Charlotte tilted her hips to accommodate him. "My body awaits only you."

Ahmose positioned the head of his cock at her entrance and thrust forward. They both cried out at the exquisite torture.

"I have dreamt of this moment, since the day you vanished," he gritted out.

"My body has longed for your touch," she gasped.

"Well, wait no longer." With that Ahmose thrust again, spearing her deep.

Charlotte rose up to meet each gliding movement, her pussy gripping him in an intimate embrace. He sank inside her warmth, plunging possessively in and out, merging with her as only man and woman could. As one they moved, hot flesh upon flesh, leading each other on a journey of completion.

The familiar ache started low in her body, winding tighter and tighter. Charlotte couldn't get close enough or feel him deep enough to satisfy her endless need. After fearing she'd never hold him again, her need was desperate, urgent—frantic. She bucked her hips with each thrust of his cock, until the sensation was too much. Charlotte cried out, climaxing in a fiery explosion of ecstasy. Ahmose followed her descent into oblivion, his hips jerking as his seed spilled from his body into hers.

They lay side by side for several minutes, enjoying the intimacy. When they finally floated back down to reality, Ahmose leaned over and kissed her tenderly.

"I've got someone I'd like you to meet," she whispered against his mouth.

Ahmose braced himself on one elbow, his face quizzical.

Charlotte grabbed his hand. Slowly she brought it to her flat stomach. Ahmose frowned for but a moment then broke out into a smile that could have been seen from the heavens.

"You bring me great joy, my love." He beamed. "Just promise me one thing." Ahmose grabbed her hand and slid the gold ring she'd dropped at Karnak, back on her finger.

"What is that?"

His grin widened. "That you'll stay by my side and we'll rule the kingdoms of Egypt together."

"I promise," Charlotte laughed, slipping her hands around his neck.

"From your lips," he kissed her again, "to our son Amenhotep's ears." Ahmose leaned down and pressed his lips to her flat abdomen.

She was home.

Epilogue

Upon the death of his brother, King Kamose, Ahmose I became pharaoh and went on to unite the kingdoms of Egypt, fulfilling his destiny. A feat many remarked would never have occurred without his lovely wife, Charlotte, the bearer of the Tears of Amun, by his side.

Their years were filled with happiness and much love, bringing into the world ten children — seven daughters and three sons. One of which, Amenhotep, would go on to become a great pharaoh, following in his father's footsteps.

Why an electronic book?

We live in the Information Age — an exciting time in the history of human civilization in which technology rules supreme and continues to progress in leaps and bounds every minute of every hour of every day. For a multitude of reasons, more and more avid literary fans are opting to purchase e-books instead of paperbacks. The question to those not yet initiated to the world of electronic reading is simply: why?

1. Price. *An electronic title at Ellora's Cave Publishing runs anywhere from 40-75% less than the cover price of the <u>exact same title</u> in paperback format. Why? Cold mathematics. It is less expensive to publish an e-book than it is to publish a paperback, so the savings are passed along to the consumer.*

2. Space. *Running out of room to house your paperback books? That is one worry you will never have with electronic novels. For a low one-time cost, you can purchase a handheld computer designed specifically for e-reading purposes. Many e-readers are larger than the average handheld, giving you plenty of screen room. Better yet, hundreds of titles can be stored within your new library — a single microchip. (Please note that Ellora's Cave does not endorse any specific brands. You can check our website at* www.ellorascave.com *for customer recommendations we make available to new consumers.)*

3. Mobility. *Because your new library now consists of only a microchip, your entire cache of books can be taken with you wherever you go.*

4. Personal preferences are accounted for. *Are the words you are currently reading too small? Too* large? *Too...***ANNOYING***? Paperback books cannot be modified according to personal preferences, but e-books can.*
5. Innovation. *The way you read a book is not the only advancement the Information Age has gifted the literary community with. There is also the factor of what you can read. Ellora's Cave Publishing will be introducing a new line of interactive titles that are available in e-book format only.*
6. Instant gratification. *Is it the middle of the night and all the bookstores are closed? Are you tired of waiting days — sometimes weeks — for online and offline bookstores to ship the novels you bought? Ellora's Cave Publishing sells instantaneous downloads 24 hours a day, 7 days a week, 365 days a year. Our e-book delivery system is 100% automated, meaning your order is filled as soon as you pay for it.*

Those are a few of the top reasons why electronic novels are displacing paperbacks for many an avid reader. As always, Ellora's Cave Publishing welcomes your questions and comments. We invite you to email us at service@ellorascave.com or write to us directly at: P.O. Box 787, Hudson, Ohio 44236-0787.

Printed in the United States
17161LVS00002B/156